AMISH HERITAGE
BY
Piper Forrest & Lily Simmons

Amish Heritage

Quilted Hills, Volume 2

Piper Forrest and Lily Simmons

Published by Bev Haynes, 2019.

PROLOGUE

Miriam Lapp swayed back and forth in the wicker rocker on the front porch of her family home. She fled the well-wishers who filled the large house. The funeral for her grandmother, Sadie Lapp, concluded three hours ago and still the members of their district hung around. *Go home. Go home.* The words resonated through her mind as she willed the people away. Yes, they were giving their kindness, but Miriam needed the space to think without worrying about someone coming to her and derailing her thoughts.

Miriam reached under the neckline of her dress and pulled out the healing bag her grandmother gave her, moments before she died. The woman took it from around her neck and placed it on Miriam's. From the time she was a toddler, the old woman worked with Miriam, teaching her about healing, and herbs. The last thing to happen, *Mammi* said, was when she passed on, Miriam became the keeper of the necklace, which she would always wear, never was it to be removed from her until she passed it on herself.

Miriam helped Mammi make a new leather strap last year, keeping the worn one in place while putting the new one through the bone circles at each side of the bag. Once the leather was secure, Miriam snipped the old strip, folded it, and placed it in the wooden box her grandmother took from her ancient hope chest. In the box were many straps indicating many generations of healers in her family.

The small bag felt more substantial to her somehow. Was it actually? Or was it the weight of the knowledge she soon had to fill *Mammi's* shoes?

The thoughts overwhelmed her. Was she ready for this? Miriam sighed, stood, and walked to the door to enter the living room. Fear and trepidation were for another day. Today, she was the *Braucherei.*

CHAPTER 1

Levi Miller unhooked his trotting horse from the buggy inside the large barn. He'd returned from his ride through three districts checking out horses for sale.

Last month, Levi sold two beautiful standardbred horses he'd trained, getting them up to speed on the racetrack between the barn and the back-fence line, preparing them to pull a cart and to both trot and pace in the Amish chariot races held in Pennsylvania. He needed at least two more horses to begin training. Building his herd took time and much study.

Coming from a family of farmers, Levi enjoyed working with animals more than growing crops. After completing his eighth-grade education, he worked two years with his father on the farm, but his heart was not in it. He spoke to the Bishop and to his father to gain permission to work with Jeremiah Schmidt on his horse ranch which was twenty miles to the west of Paradise Wells.

Levi lived behind Jeremiah's house in the *dawdi haus* and ate meals with the Schmidt family as payment for his work. He stayed with the family for five years until he turned twenty-one.

Meeting Miriam Lapp again at her sister's shop over two years ago, they courted one year and married a year later. Levi smiled as he finished brushing down his horse, Luca. The time was getting on to late afternoon and in October, evening came earlier than it had during the long days of summer. He smelled the dried leaves under the trees and smiled. The busy summer was ending. He breathed deeply and noted onion and spices in the air.

Anxiously, he put up the brush and left the horse stall, bringing down the wooden latch to secure the horse for the night. Married for only a year, Levi could hardly wait to give his bride a big hug and a kiss. He asked her to go along today, but she served so many customers at the store this time of the year, and she didn't want to lose sales. The store belonged to her sister, Ruby, but Miriam ran it for her. Ruby had her hands full running the farm stay.

As he closed the barn doors, Levi heard a horse and buggy approach at a breakneck speed. *What in the world?* The racket was close, but no one came toward the barn, which he thought odd. Stripping off his leather work gloves, he ran his hand through his bowl cut black hair. Something didn't feel right, and his stomach squeezed nervously thinking of Miriam alone in the house.

Stepping more quickly, Levi was halfway to the house when he saw an open buggy racing down the narrow road in front of his home. The horse and buggy threw dirt in the air, but he could tell Miriam was with the man. They rounded the corner, and he lost sight of them.

Levi rushed into the house to see if there had been a disruption or some sign of who had been there, but nothing. A stew sat on the propane-powered stove. The fire was off, so Miriam had the sense to do that, but why did she take off with the man?

The only reason he could come up with was, his wife Miriam was the area healer woman and midwife. The *Braucherei.*

Levi watched the sun flood the field with color. "Where are you, my love?" He pushed off the porch rail. Miriam has been gone for two days. "Not a word."

Levi walked to clear away some of his anger and fear, but it did not help. He did not like the emotions which flooded his senses over Miriam. What if she was hurt? This was his biggest concern. He hoped Ruby held some answers.

"Levi, you two have been married for over a year. You understand how some of these midwife calls go. *Boppli* come in their own time."

"*Jah*, but I should know where she is. Miriam always tells me if a little one is near, so I do not worry."

"I agree with you. Somehow this is different. Sit down and have a cup of *kaffe* with me. Have you eaten breakfast? There are a few slices of bacon left, and I can scramble some eggs."

"*Jah*, fantastic, I am hungry."

Ruby went to the gas-powered refrigerator and took out the left-over bacon and three eggs. "Just relax. I am sure Miriam will be home soon, and you will hear the full story of what happened. These are just experiences you will have to get used to, Levi." She broke the eggs into a bowl and whipped them with a fork, then poured them into the hot pan.

"I worry about her. Her kind heart keeps her from thinking through her actions." He paced while Ruby cooked. "What if she doesn't come home soon? How long should I wait?"

Ruby plated up the food and pointed to a chair at the large table in the middle of her kitchen. "I am not sure what to tell you. I would wait until the afternoon to tell Bishop Eischler. Oh! Levi! I can call her number on my cell phone. I am sure the bishop would let you buy one since Miriam travels a distance at times. If she faced a problem, she could call you. Why did you not called her from your phone shanty?"

Ruby caught him looking down at the floor. The skin between his eyebrows pulled into a frown. "Because I do not have her number. I was angry she had the phone. I threw the piece of paper away.

"Levi! You should not have done that. What if she needed you and cannot contact you at the shanty?"

Just as she said this, her phone rang. The sound of wind chimes reverberated behind her apron in the dress pocket. Setting the plate in front of Levi, she answered, "Troyer Farm Stay. This is Ruby."

Ruby touched Levi's shoulder to get his attention. Then pointing to the phone, she mouthed *Miriam*. She pulled the phone away from her ear and pressed the screen to allow speakerphone. "Miriam, Levi is here with me. You are on speakerphone, so both of us can hear your voice. Where are you? Levi has been so worried."

Miriam spoke slowly, "I'm over in the district to the west of ours with the Miller family. Mrs. Miller just had twin daughters. It was a struggle to get everyone through it all. I was calling to have you contact Levi, but I can hear it is not necessary."

Levi broke into the conversation. "You are gone too long, Miriam. Why did you not tell me where you were going and for how long? I worry about you."

"Levi, I left you a note on the table. Didn't you find it?"

"*Nee*. I saw nothing, but I will look for it. When will you come home?"

"It shouldn't be too much longer. I'm waiting for Mr. Miller to bring me back. I believe all of us are worn down to nubs, Levi. I'm sorry you did not find my note, but the man was in a dreadful hurry to get me to his wife. If he had not come so soon, I fear we would have lost all three of them."

"I will come and pick you up, where is this place?"

After Miriam gave the details, Ruby remembered Levi had walked here, just over a mile from his and Miriam's horse ranch. "I'll let Levi take my buggy, and he can bring it and the horse back home with him tomorrow. Let's get you home for some rest."

CHAPTER 2

Levi traveled over two hours from Paradise Wells. It was a long distance his Miriam had gone. Was there no midwife for this district?

Following the directions given to him before he left, he saw the turn. It was barely a path with weeds overgrown and deep ruts. It did not appear the landowner took care of the property. It was not very Amish. The plain people took great care in their properties.

Wondering how to find the house through the dense foliage, he was lost until the horse stepped through an opening and before him, stood a dilapidated house. It was large, which was the only thing it had going for it. He'd seen shacks in better repair. Miriam had been called to this place? It did not look as if anyone lived there. The area screamed poverty. Suddenly, he understood Miriam's desire to help. These people needed all the help they could get. Maybe he had been a bachelor too long, waiting until his thirties to marry Miriam. She was older as well and, at times, they butted heads over silly thoughts, each wanting their own way. He smiled. Miriam had his heart.

Just as those thoughts filled his mind, a man stepped out onto the crooked porch. The tall, thin man looked familiar. Maybe Levi had known him in the past before he was married and wore his beard.

A hitching rail stood under a large shade tree, and Levi guided the horse in that direction. A trough of water was nearby, so he had no fear for Ruby's horse. With rest and drink, recovery was in store for the horse.

"Levi. I am happy you are here. I want you to realize your wife saved my wife, Anna and our twin *boppli*."

Levi squinted his eyes. *Wayne*. He could not believe his eyes. His stomach leaped, and his heart filled with joy. "Brother! I have found you after all this time." Levi offered his hand, and as Wayne grasped it, Levi pulled it and the man into his arms. "*Ach*, I have missed you, big brother." The man smelled of sweat and soiled clothing, but Levi was not going to let it deter him from his joy over seeing his brother.

"I never wanted you to see me living like this, Levi, but since the shunning, there has not been a way for us to recover."

Levi shook his head. "*Nee*. If I had known, my help was yours. Let's not speak of this now. I want to see my new nephews? Or...nieces?"

"Nieces. We haven't named them yet. Anna and I can't make up our minds." With a laugh, Wayne placed his hand on Levi's back and led him toward the house.

The only sounds surrounding Miriam and Levi were the clip-clop of the horse's hooves on the oiled highway. Levi drove the buggy close to the side of the road, and occasionally, the horse kicked up dirt when he encroached the weeded edges.

Levi did not have words to offer his wife. His heart tightened in his chest when the thoughts of her lying to him screamed through his mind. Miriam knew he missed his brother, and he had no idea where Wayne had got off to since he had been shunned. She knew where he lived, and she had not said a word.

What caused her to act this way? He assumed they shared everything, and there were no secrets between them. How wrong could he have been?

Miriam turned toward him. He felt her slight movement, but he kept his eyes forward, much like the horse in front of him who wore blinders.

"Please speak to me, husband," Miriam uttered softly.

Levi heard the sadness as it played at the corners of her words. She possessed a way to reach his heart, but this time, he guarded his emotions. Miriam must learn he was the head of their household and could not keep things from him. And she certainly could not run off without telling him where she was going and with whom.

"Levi."

He tried not to reply but found himself uttering aloud, "What?"

"I want to explain. It is not fair for you to treat me like this."

Knowing Miriam as he did, he knew her movements meant she had crossed her arms under her bosom. She was firing up for a big pout. Somehow, when she turned all of this around, it would become his fault. *I suppose I must answer her or suffer for it later.*

"What?"

Miriam had her healing bag in her hand. It was a sure indication she was upset as she kept the item under her clothing, not exposed unless she needed it to heal. He supposed she was using it for herself today. He felt his heart softening to the situation. A sigh burst from her lips. "Over the months, I did not realize that Anna's husband was your brother."

Levi turned his head and gave her a glance. "How did you get all this way for her appointments without me knowing about it? Did Wayne come for you each time?"

"*Nee,* Anna drove out to our place. I thought she always came alone. I just recently found out your brother waited for her to return to town. I had no idea they lived so far away. I had no idea the man was your brother."

He snapped the reins as the horse slowed. Levi wanted nothing more than to be home and have a strong cup of *kaffe.* "When did you find out about my brother?"

The fall afternoon sun hid behind a cloud, and Levi felt his wife shiver. "Cover up with a blanket. You do not need to take a chill." Levi was softening even more as he listened to his wife's story. If she did not know Wayne was his brother, then it was not a lie. "Tell me why you didn't come out to the barn the other night before you left with Wayne."

"I did not know you were home. That is why I left you a note on the table. I wrote it to catch your attention."

"*Nee* Miriam. I did not find a note. I left the barn when I heard a buggy, but you were flying down the road by the time I got to the house. It scared the life out of me. Then you didn't come home the next day. What was I to think?" He snapped the reins in his hands to move the horse closer to the side of the road as a car passed them. "You still haven't answered me. When did you realize this father was my brother?"

Instead of hearing soft, reassuring words from his wife, Levi's head jerked back at her answer. "Well, if you carried a cell phone as I do, we would not have this problem, right?"

Here we go. My wife feels it is all my fault. "Miriam, the only reason the Bishop lets you have your phone is so if you need it for medical work, you have a way to contact people, I have no reason for one."

"You do!" Miriam's voice rose an octave and pierced his ear closest to her. "If I need you to help me, or go for the medical doctor in town…"

Levi shook his head. He might have to give in to her, but right at this moment, he just wanted to think about his brother and family living in a shack. And all the others he saw, or Wayne spoke of.

"You still have not answered my question about Wayne. When did you know?"

"Please, I am getting a headache from all this. We can talk about it later. Hopefully, we should be home in less than thirty minutes."

He shook his head in dismay. Why? Why not tell him? "Please, just answer me."

"Will you believe me?"

"Of course, I'll believe you. Why do you even ask this of me?"

"Because you are in a mood. You just want to take the negative stance about everything I say." She sighed and continued. "Alright, I'll tell you. I learned of it late last night while birthing her babies, Anna called out her husband's name. Suddenly, I put the names together and realized these people were your family."

Miriam kept her arms crossed and never said another word to him as they rode along.

Levi's mind filled with ways to help Wayne. Every thought brought him back to problems He even feared asking about getting a cell phone. He had to know where Miriam was. Until then, worry filled him.

CHAPTER 3

Ruby watched Levi drive away in her buggy. She had never seen him so upset. He and her sister had been married a year. Surely, he was used to her erratic schedule by now. Miriam was the midwife for more than just their district. If need be, she went long distances to help people. Ruby loved Levi, but he could be a bit harsh. But then Miriam could be introverted and keep things to herself. She shook her head. They might figure out their relationship over the years.

Of course, there was the tradition of their family as *Braucherei.* The powwow healers. The practice became faded over the years, but the old people in the community embraced Miriam and called on her to carry on the tradition. Wart removal. Nausea relief. Depression. Miriam coddled the old folks, and they loved her for it.

Ruby sighed. Their *Mammi* and her sister had been so close, and the healing modality from years past had bound them. Now, Miriam was married, and she couldn't just go off without telling Levi her intentions.

Moving from the window with her thoughts, Ruby began making *kaffe*, then took out the doughnuts she made for the gathering. Carly, Hannah, and she were going over the final plans for Hannah and Matthew's wedding. In two weeks, her son would be a married man. Ruby shook her head. Matthew wearing a beard? Amazing.

So many things had changed over the past few months. Carly Laine became their long-term guest. Ruby enjoyed her company so much. Imagine. An Englischer living in the farm stay. Ruby wondered at times if Carly acted more Amish than Englisch? Smiling to herself, she watched the color of the liquid change to dark brown through the glass knob of the stovetop *kaffe* pot. Turning off the gas, Ruby pulled the large container toward her, grabbed a mug, and poured herself a delicious brew. She was ready for the girls to arrive.

Carly Laine paused and listened from her apartment at the farm stay. Her friend, Ruby, was up and working in the kitchen.

She smiled, it felt so lovely to be part of this family. If someone told her she would live with the Amish, she would laugh over the announcement. She loved living at the farm stay. Carly had booked a two-week stay which was almost five months ago, now she was a permanent renter.

She knew the new apartment was all Matthew and Hannah's plan, and they worked so hard to make it so. Together, they changed the large rooms, hall, and bathroom at the end of the living quarters on the second floor into a beautiful apartment for her to rent. The young couple laughed through the work and proclaimed it as *fun!*

Three large windows looked out over the fields, which were golden in their fall colors. With the inner wall gone, the living area was extensive with one door to the private bathroom and the other entrance to the stairs leading to the kitchen. One wall separated her apartment from the guest bedrooms.

Her new quilt from Ruby's store grazed the full bed in all its design and wintery blue colors. Miriam worked at the store nearly every day, and she was an expert at selling the items. The quilt had been expensive, but Miriam made her a good deal, and now it graced her bed.

Carly couldn't wipe her smile away. She made sure Matthew approve her colors and wallpaper. His words "calm for the Englisch" with a wink. He and Hannah both liked how it came out. She overheard the two talking about switching to apartments in the future.

"All in the dreams of being in love and starting their lives."

At this moment, everything was settling down in her life.

Carly felt like giggling when she heard Ruby call up the stairs for her to come down. She took a long look at her home and headed down to join Ruby and Hannah for the wedding planning.

"...and, the celery is kept in the large wash tubs that Matthew setup." Hannah's face glowed with radiance after her last announcement.

Ruby swallowed. She could not say a word. This planning was stressful as Hannah went about things differently than Ruby did. Now she understood the comments her friends made about being a mother-in-law and having to bite her tongue.

Carly caught Ruby's eye and smiled reassuringly at her then said, "Hannah, I see you brought your notebook. How many people do you have coming?" Ruby knew Carly tried to keep it light and give her a chance to calm down.

"At least two hundred with the children, I suspect there will be more, so we should plan on two hundred fifty."

Carly spoke up, "so we need to increase the meat a bit?"

Hannah twirled the strings on her *Kapp* in a nervous manner. "Ruby, I will ask *Daed* to buy more chickens. Do you suppose *kinner* will eat more of the chicken dish rather than a slice of meat?"

Ruby gave a devious smile at Carly. "I do have a huge range sitting behind us. If I gave you the recipe and instructions, do you suppose you could cook the extra casseroles here?"

Carly chimed in, "Sure, I can do the casseroles here as I'll be cooking for the in-house guests anyway."

Hannah agreed, and so did Ruby.

"I thought you might put up a fuss, Carly." Ruby laughed. "You sure did when I had you cook by yourself the first time."

"I've learned a lot in the last few months. Besides, I really do like to cook, and it feels good to be doing it again. You know, baking has become my true love, though."

"It is a good thing you do with all this going on. I don't know what I might have done without you, for sure and for certain."

"I think we have things settled; I feel good about the food for all. Thank you both for all your help." Hannah smiled. "I understand I'm not much of a chef. I hope to learn from both of you. How long do you think it will take me?"

Ruby and Carly's gazes met across the table, in a warning to each other to not make the girl feel offended. They knew it would take a long time, if ever.

"I have reservations for your family staying here, Hannah." Ruby avoided answering Hannah's question and hoped the girl did not notice.

"I'm so glad you are offering the farm stay free to them, Ruby. They must travel a long way to come to the wedding. *Daed* will have families with children at our house. And thank you too, Carly, for offering to share your room with me the night before. That way I can give my room to our family."

"Is your father's new barn done and ready for your wedding service?" Carly asked.

"Yes, it is ready to be set up for the service and then the food. *Daed* even has the big heater coming this week. He is excited. I think it is more for the coming winter when he has to work in the cold barn rather than for the wedding." She laughed easily.

"How long did you say the service lasted?" Carly looked at Hannah.

Ruby filled in the answer when Hannah looked lost. "Three hours for the service, then the vows are spoken. Then we set up to eat." She reached over and closed her hand over Hannah's nervous movement.

"It will be fine, dear," Ruby said, "All brides get nervous over all the planning, not to mention the thoughts of being married and all the responsibilities that it brings to you. You will do well."

"I love you both," Hannah spoke softly. "With my mother gone to heaven, my *daed* couldn't do all of this for me. You two will be grandmothers to our children."

"Grandmother, hmm, how about Auntie?" They all laughed over Carly's declaration.

The nip in the air made Carly pull her sweater tighter around her. She looked at the darkening clouds and knew snow was coming soon. Worrying about the wedding, she spoke under her breath, "All those people are going to freeze before they eat."

She wanted to laugh over the meeting they all just finished at Ruby's. Carly could feel the dilemma flowing through her friend, Ruby. It wasn't easy to watch your child grow away from you. She had a feeling the babies from Matthew and Hannah would fill the emptiness in her friend.

Carly examined her own status with Asher. Could they make it work again? He began the new job of Chief of Police in Paradise Wells and asked her to be his deputy. Carly realized she hadn't seen him in over a week. It was a big job and very demanding, even in a small area.

She knew Asher well enough to understand he had a lot on his mind. *No. I won't take the job, heck we wouldn't see each other if I did.*

Carly admitted the decision she reached came from a lot more than seeing Asher. For the first time in her life, she felt at peace. The thought of going back to police or private investigating left her feeling cold. To experience this field of work again would wipe out all she came to be, here, here in this beautiful country setting with the Amish.

She bit her lip knowing Asher gave her more time than he did anyone else for the deputy job. She had to provide him with her final decision. Carly told him last night on the phone that she would give him an answer today. She made the decision and felt as if she could breathe again. Carly hoped this was the right thing to do, and he would understand her reasoning.

She kicked at a mound of dirt and laughed softly. This worry had to be pushed aside because the wedding came first. What a huge affair. She didn't see how they did it all.

Carly decided the two of them, Hannah and Ruby, were both a wreck over this wedding and all that goes with it. She had never seen so much celery as there was in the basement cellar.

It felt good to laugh over it. One of the perks of living here was all this openness. She could walk in the open air and let herself work things out without someone seeing. This is an excellent place to live.

Her finger punched at the phone's buttons. "Come on, Asher, pick up the phone! Twenty-eight chickens, who cooks so many chickens!" she took a deep breath and tried to calm down, but it was useless. "Why won't he answer? I need to know what to do."

She'd never touched the slimy things like livers. How in the world could she get all this made?

Finally, she disconnected the call and jammed the cell phone into her back pocket. Why hadn't she told Ruby her misgivings in the first place instead of blindly agreeing to cook extra casseroles? Ruby thought she was onboard, but heck, she was scared to death. All she could imagine was a cover of a book she'd read when she was a kid. It had a picture of a witch on the front cover stirring this big cauldron. Yes, that was how she felt.

Carly went in the laundry room to wash the linens. There on top of the dryer set four huge pans. She shook her head; this was a disaster. She needed someone to tell her what to do.

Her phone vibrated in her pocket. She snatched it out and saw it was Ash calling her back.

"Ash! Where have you been, I need help."

"Hey girl, calm down and tell me what happened."

"Chickens. Twenty-eight to be exact, and five dozen eggs and all those awful innards stuffed inside!"

She could hear him laughing and wanted to reach through the line and shake him silly. "It isn't funny, Asher. I don't know how to cook like this."

"It is the wedding casserole. It is okay, Carly. You don't have to cook it all, the other ladies will help and do a pan a piece, and then you will do some. The chickens and other ingredients will begin to show up for you to make your pans."

"Really? Don't try to fool me, Ash. Just tell me how to get it done."

"I just did. I used to watch my mom cook it for weddings."

"Maybe I'll give you a call when all this begins arriving!"

"I don't think so...I'm sure to be busy and on a call,"

She could hear Asher snorting in the background as she pulled the phone away from her ear.

"You are really pushing it, mister."

He only laughed harder on the other end.

She could hear him start... "Livers, and gizzards and hearts, oh my!"

CHAPTER 4

The clatter of the wind-up alarm clock barely penetrated Ruby's consciousness. She tried to open her eyes, but the sensation was like thick wool clogging her brain and burning her eyelids. Sleep evaded her last night, and she tossed and turned for hours. The last time she looked at the clock, it read one a.m. Now it was five.

Reaching out her hand from under the warm quilt, she tapped the button on top of the clock, shutting it down. The sun was not up yet, and with her shade pulled across the window, it was much darker in the room.

Today was her son Matthew's wedding day. She had so much to do, and here she was, having a hard time rolling out of her bed. She told David, Hannah's father and her next-door neighbor, that she would be there to help organize the kitchen. Hannah had no mother to help her with the wedding as she died before the family moved to this district.

Hannah's three aunts and uncles plus children were staying with the Fisher family, and Ruby agreed to meet them at five-thirty. On that note, Ruby threw her legs over the edge of the bed, then stood. The braided rug kept her feet from freezing when they touched the floor. November in Pennsylvania became cold at night. Before she could move on to getting dressed, though, she needed her slippers. Rummaging around with her toes, she found them and slid them on.

It didn't take long for her morning ritual, and once finished, she exited the bathroom into a small hallway which was between the two bedrooms. The *dawdi haus* had a small living room and an efficiency kitchen with small appliances. Quickly she fixed *kaffe* in the percolator then set it on the stove and turned the propane to high. It took only a short time making it this way.

Special days like this brought the memory of her husband back to her mind. He'd been gone to *Gott* for many years, but the pain of his loss still hurt her heart. She smiled. Her husband was not there, but she felt his pride in their son.

Ruby sat at the small table as she waited for the *kaffe* and drummed her fingers on the wooden top. Once she knew the wedding was up-coming, she traded Matthew living spaces. He needed a large bedroom in the house to bring his bride. After all, he was the legal owner of the farm stay. Ruby signed over the land and business to him as he was the head of their household. She continued as hostess and to cook at the big house, but she knew she had to pull away once Hannah got a feel for the business. Heaven only knew what she would do once it happened. At thirty-seven, Ruby felt too young to be considered an old person. Possibly she could create a business out of her knitting and crochet.

Her new daughter-in-law as of this day worked at the farm stay, and Ruby felt the younger woman would have no problem dropping into the role she had created over the years since her husband's death.

The aroma of the finished brew reached her and drew her from her thoughts. Standing, she moved to the counter and pulled the lid from an insulated mug. She planned to take it with her as she walked to David's home not far from hers.

As she threw on a cape over her dress and apron, Ruby glanced at the clock on the wall. She had just enough time to get there. Tardy on the wedding day? Never.

Miriam and Levi walked with Ruby to David Fisher's barn. The man kept his animals in the old barn until the wedding was over, saving his new building for Hannah's wedding. Everyone supposed he did not want one bit of hay to ruin her day.

The sky was a deep November blue with a few stray strands of clouds, but no weather threatening to ruin the day. "We couldn't have asked *Gott* for a more beautiful day for a wedding," Miriam said. There was a slight breeze stirring the fragrance of dried leaves and corn stalks in the air.

"*Jah,* I feared for all these people stranded here in a blizzard. I could not imagine how to feed them all for days on end," Ruby said.

Levi took his wife's hand saying, "I expect to see you fluttering here and there as you help in the makeshift kitchen near the back of the barn once the service is over. I will catch up with you when things calm down."

"If we're lucky, we may get to sit before serving supper!" Miriam laughed.

As they reached the wide-open barn door, the threesome separated with Levi moving toward the men's side of the barn, and Miriam and Ruby to the women's area.

Miriam smiled as she watched her husband walk away. It felt so good to have lost the tension between them if only for a moment. Her heart softened when she recalled his sheepish grin after returning home from Wayne and Anna's shack only to find her note sitting on the table with the sugar bowl on top of it. But the disagreement regarding Levi's brother Wayne and his family moving to their home caused a big gap between her and Levi. Miriam knew the family needed a place of safety and warmth the shack they squatted in did not provide but did it have to be her and Levi's home? But if not them, then who would take them? Levi assured her there must be a family to take them in. What a relief this thought had been. She chastised herself for thinking of it as the service began.

She followed Ruby to sit on the first row facing the wedding couple and their attendants. It was an area saved for the family. Across the way, David and his younger children sat. David waved at Ruby. She had spent the past few months helping Hannah organize the wedding and had kept the father of the bride calmer. The man was a basket case.

Ruby's face is glowing with a blush. *My goodness. Does my dear sister have a man interested in her?* Miriam pondered. They were both around the same age, and they were both single because their spouses died.

Returning her thoughts away from romance, she noticed Hannah had selected a robin-egg blue color for her dress and Matthew's vest. Their attendants, Matthew's best friend, John Bieler and his wife Susan wore a more luxurious version of the color. They were the only bright notes in the vast space. The men in the congregation wore black trousers and vests with white shirts, and the women wore subdued darker colored dresses.

Bishop Eischler and his three ministers approached the front of the congregation and silence ensued over the more than two hundred individuals.

Miriam bowed her head as the prayer was led by the first minister. Each man had a particular portion of the service to deliver. At the end of the three hours, Bishop Eischler would call Matthew and Hannah to stand with their attendants and exchange their vows.

As the service went on, Miriam remembered her wedding just over a year ago when she married Levi. Sadness overtook her when thoughts of the tension in their home came back to her. There was nothing she could do to change things. The biggest problem was, Wayne was banned from the district. Of course, it was the old Bishop who had done it, but still, he did have a reason. Wayne could not give up drinking. She and Levi noticed Wayne had not imbibed so his affinity to drink must have passed.

Levi had not told her if his brother was coming and if so which family was taking them in. All she did was worry. If she spoke to her brother-in-law, she worried about her shunning, and then, the impossibility to see her patients as they could have nothing to do with her and risk being shunned themselves. What a nightmare. She had to give Levi credit for offering to help his brother's family.

Suddenly, she realized the Bishop was calling the wedding couple to the front, along with their attendants. In a very brief time, Matthew and Hannah had exchanged their vows, and the two couples turned to leave the barn.

Miriam looked over at Ruby when she heard a soft sob play in her sister's chest. She reached over and squeezed Ruby's arm in support. "It is okay, sister. You now have a daughter and the hopes of *boppli* in your life again."

"You are right, but at this moment, I feel as if life, as I have lived, is ending. I am not sure what I will do with myself."

"We need to make ourselves useful in the kitchen area. The men want to turn these benches into tables."

They walked toward the back of the barn and met Carly coming toward them with a large pan of chicken casserole. "Some woman in the house told me to bring the casserole out here, and I'm to serve it and make sure not to run out. Where does it need to go?"

Ruby laughed at her friend. "*Jah*. Over to the steam table. See it? It's the long metal table with holes in it. Put the pan into a hole. The easiest one is at the end. You will be able to get out of there easily to go to the house for another pan. Be sure not to run out. Just ask the woman next to you to serve the casserole while you are getting another pan."

Miriam looked at the two women and had to refrain from laughing. Carly looked scared to death, and she knew her friend was afraid. The detective was out of her element. A true friend of the Amish the *Englischer* was. And loved by both she and Ruby. Even the whole district.

Watching Carly serving the casserole, she took in the interaction the woman had with the community and the others from a distance. She was accepted by all of them. A very unusual happening between the

Amish and Englisch. Yes, Carly seemed to have found a home here in Paradise Wells district.

Ruby stayed busy all afternoon. Being with the other women serving the first meal, then the evening meal was a delight. At the moment, her feet were killing her.

The highlight of the afternoon came about when Mrs. Eischler cut her finger while slicing a cake. Bleeding everywhere, she called out for some help. Of course, Mammi Schultz, who appeared to be in her nineties, called out for Miriam to perform a healing.

Because she was the bishop's wife, the woman protested to no avail. Miriam took over in moments, rinsing Mrs. Eischler's finger under cold water, then she placed a towel over the wound. Wrapping her fingers around Mrs. Eischler's, Miriam closed her eyes and focused on her healing.

Mrs. Eischler sat in the chair someone placed behind her and gave in to the healing.

Miriam stayed in her trance-like state for nearly fifteen minutes. Suddenly, she opened her eyes, removed the towel, and looked at the wound. Nothing was there. Not even a red line remained.

"*Awk!* Miriam! Just look what you have done!"

Bishop Eischler, hearing his wife's cries, raced into the room. "What is happening here?" His voice stern with a deep rumble asked.

All the ladies backed away, leaving Miriam and Mrs. Eischler in the middle of the room. The bishop looked at the two women expectantly.

"She healed me! Look!" The woman shook her finger in her husband's face. "She really is a healer!"

The bishop's face paled. "You are sure, wife?"

Ruby felt her heart plunge to her stomach. The devout religious community paid little attention to her family's healing skills, but to have it shoved in their faces today might cause a rift between them.

"*Jah!* Ask any of the others. They saw it. I was bleeding badly. Look." She reached in the sink and pulled out a blood-covered towel.

The bishop's eyes narrowed at Miriam for a moment. He said, "As long as you are alright, I'll leave you all to your work." He turned and went out the door to the outside. His face was still pale, but Ruby hoped the cold air would revive him.

A couple of hours later, knowing not much was going on in the house, Ruby slipped away and ambled into the back-porch door of David's house. If only she were able to sit for a bit. She was exhausted. Passing through the kitchen, she reached the large living room. Near the fire was a sturdy wooden rocking chair with a lap quilt folded across the arm.

Ruby sat and placed her feet on a small ottoman in front of the chair. In moments her eyes were closed.

The muffled sound of someone stoking a fire brought Ruby out of her sleep, and she slowly awoke. David knelt before the fire and got the logs burning again.

"Good evening, sleepy head," David said quietly to Ruby.

Ruby's eyes flew open at his words, and she slid her feet off the ottoman and to the floor. With this movement, she sat bolt upright in the chair,

"*Ach!* What time is it, David?" She looked toward a window and saw it was dark outside,

David rose from the fire and looked down into her eyes. "It's nearly six."

"Oh, I must go help with supper!"

"*Nee...* it's all taken care of. All the company is either gone, or the few remaining stragglers are all in their rooms. David and Hannah are at the farm stay. Do not worry about yourself. It is under control."

"I must get back to my little home. Make sure everyone is accounted for. Also, see if they need anything."

"Isn't this what you have Carly doing?"

"Well, yes, but it never hurts to be on hand..."

"*Nee*...it only serves to make the person into a nervous wreck and afraid to make any decisions at all."

Ruby nodded, took David's proffered arm, and walked with him into the kitchen. After their *kaffe* and a plate of wedding casserole, David walked Ruby back to her *dawdi haus*. Turning toward David after she stepped up onto the small covered porch, she said, "Thank you for all you have done with the wedding. I am glad all our problems are over. We did not have the best of meetings some months ago." Ruby smiled guiltily.

"*Nee,* we did not, but it is in the past. Ruby, I consider you my best friend."

Ruby was glad the night was dark, and there were no lights on inside because she felt her face flush. This man made her heart pound with excitement. Her breath caught in her throat.

"*Jah,* I have felt like your friend. I am glad you are mine."

David made no comment for a moment, then he looked directly at her and bid her goodnight.

Ruby stood on the porch watching him go until the darkness of the night closed around him, and he disappeared into its depths. She sighed, and turned, opening her door and stepping inside. It was strange the feeling sweeping over her. She felt lonely and a bit sad.

CHAPTER 5

Miriam drove the buggy along the dirt path leading from the highway. Both she and Ruby had decided to close the store for the week of the wedding. Today, Saturday was her last day free of the store work. Monday would find her back at work. She shook her head. Never did she feel this way. It was not the Amish way to dislike their jobs, whether it was in their homes or at a business or trade.

The buggy wheel fell into a hole and jolted her from her thoughts. She needed to speak to Levi about fixing the holes in the road from the highway up to their house as they used it every day at this time of the year. Today the short distance exhausted her with each bounce.

It was a good thing she had been away from work because an older woman had a difficult birth, and Miriam spent the sum of two days with her. She had not headed home until the roosters were welcoming the district to morning. Once the *boppli* was settled, after midnight, thoughts of her comfortable, warm bed, even for a few hours, materialized before her and she decided to drive home.

Levi was up and making *kaffe* when she dragged in, and he pointed her toward the bedroom with a kiss on the tip of her nose.

Miriam slept until noon. Bless Levi. He knew how tired she was. Even with all the sleep, she was exhausted and only fixed chicken noodle soup and grilled cheese sandwiches for supper. After making short work of the dishes, she was back in her bed asleep before seven o'clock in the evening.

A week later, the November morning had been clear and crisp, and Miriam enjoyed her walk to open the store. It was only a mile. The air had invigorated her to face the day, but as the afternoon descended, she could hardly drag herself home. Beat. This was the only word which described how she felt. Again. Why had she not driven her buggy to work today?

The wind came up, and the feel of snow was in the air. Humidity gathered on the wool cloak as she wrapped it tighter around her. Rounding a bend in the road, her home came into view. Smoke from the fireplace pumped into the air and it bent as a breeze caught it. *Home.*

The sight gave her step a bit more energy. All she wanted to do was take a short nap before having to gather up leftovers from her gas refrigerator. Miriam cooked an extra-large meal yesterday in case she had to be away from home. That way, Levi did not need to starve.

Levi's handsome face shone through her mind. His black hair curling under his straw hat in the summertime. His sparkling, deep blue eyes surrounded by thick lashes and best of all, his full, pink lips. She loved this man so much.

As she neared the back of the house, she saw a horse with a flat work wagon attached. Furniture, stacked this way and every way, covered the wooden flatbed. *What in the world had Levi been up to?* She did not remember him telling her of an upcoming auction.

The house Levi built for her was large. The original home for the property was on the other side of a large field. It needed cleaning and a few repairs as it sat vacant for many years. Since Levi's parents passed.

She and Levi wanted many children to fill their new home. Six bedrooms on the second story covered a large front room, big enough for church Sunday's, a bedroom, kitchen, and mudroom. Miriam walked into the mudroom and took off her cape. With working at Ruby's store, midwifery, and healings, plus caring for her home and Levi, fatigue dogged her every step.

Her shoes were tinged with dampness, so she slid on her fluffy, warm house slippers. Voices came from the kitchen. *Company.* It was not what she needed on a night like this. She sighed and walked into the kitchen.

Wayne and Levi, each holding a *boppli* sat around the kitchen table. *What in the world were they doing here? What if the bishop saw them here?* They must have stopped for a visit before arriving at the kind family's home where Levi had arranged for them to stay. Fortifying herself with a deep gulp of air, Miriam smiled and offered, "*Wilkum* to our home."

Anna had not heard her until she spoke. "*Ach!* Miriam. You are at home. I have supper nearly ready. I hope you do not mind I took over your kitchen, and a beautiful kitchen it is. I will enjoy helping you if it is alright, and it is isn't it?"

Miriam stood there, staring at the girl. She knew from her medical information that Anna was twenty years old. My but the girl could carry on. Where did she get the breath to utter all those words?

"Thank you for doing this, Anna. I'm exhausted. I am glad to see your family. Where are you headed?" Anna turned to the stove and stirred something in a big pot that smelled heavenly.

Levi and Wayne looked nervously at Anna.

Miriam caught their strange looks and felt a sinking in the middle of her stomach.

Miriam remembered the leftovers. "Did you find the leftovers? Did they make enough for all four of us?" she asked wearily, then took a chair beside the men and *boppli*.

"I added all the leftovers from the icebox and found some potatoes and a jar of tomatoes in the basement. Biscuits are in the oven and will be ready soon. Go get washed up, and I will get the table set, and the food finished."

Miriam stood, gave her husband a sharp glare as she passed him on the way out of the kitchen. She became angrier by the minute. Levi's family were taking over her home! What about Levi's promise to her? Why was this happening?

Walking into their bedroom on the main floor, she wanted to stay there and let the rest of them have supper. She would not be good company.

She looked around the room to calm herself. Levi designed the home for them. He wanted many children, and the separation of levels, making it possible to give them privacy and quiet. If Wayne, Anna, and the *kinner* stayed here, at least there was separation.

A large bathroom, plain in style with a big tub and shower combination which was accessed from a hallway off the large living room, but near the bedroom. Their company could use it and on Sunday when they hosted services, it was handy.

The one thing Miriam loved in her bedroom was the attached small room to use as a nursery. Once *boppli* arrived, they lived close to her until they were old enough for a room upstairs.

Splashing water on her face somewhat revived her and calmed her down. If she made it through supper without screaming at Levi or falling asleep in her plate, it would be a miracle. Drying her face and hands with a scratchy towel, she was ready to return to the kitchen. The sooner she got supper over, the sooner she could talk to her husband.

Walking back into the kitchen, Miriam found Anna did indeed have the meal under control. They were all waiting supper for Mirian to join them.

Levi watched her drop onto the chair beside him. "You look exhausted. All the sleep last night did not help?"

Placing a napkin on her lap, she looked at his eyes, which held such concern for her. "It did, but the store was crazy busy today."

"I will put the kitchen in order after we eat. I want you to ready yourself for bed and sleep the whole night through," Levi said. His full lips pulled into a smile. Each side dimpled handsomely.

"Neither of you have to worry. I'll handle the kitchen. We have to pay your kindness back somehow," Anna offered.

"*Jah*, I'll help, too." Wayne offered.

Anna's laugh came out in a bark. "*Nee*, husband. You just make sure the *boppli* stay asleep. That is good enough."

Miriam was confused. "What is going on?" She looked questionably at Levi.

"Wayne, Anna, and the children are going to stay with us for a while." Miriam looked at the two small, plastic carriers which held the babies. Would she be able to sleep with the tiny ones here?

"I have Wayne and Anna in the large room upstairs at the back and the babies directly across from them," he said, and reached out for her hand, and his other one reached for his brothers. They bowed in silent prayer. Then Levi cleared his throat as a notification the prayer time was over.

Miriam could not concentrate on praying. Too many questions remained unsaid and answered. She was so busy with healing and delivering, and then there was the store. *Gott* help them all.

Looking up from the silent prayer, frowning, Miriam asked, "What will they sleep on? I have no crib."

Wayne looked up directly at Miriam. His brows knit together, and his gaze showed how uncomfortable he was. "We have two cradles for the little ones and bedding as well. We will be out of your hair as soon as we can, Miriam. We must find a place to go to. I feel your bishop might not like the shunned sharing a table and a room at your home."

Levi spoke up, "This is not the case, brother. I have talked to the Bishop." Levi gave Miriam a sideways glance. "You see since you did not join the church yet with baptism, old Bishop Yoder could not shun you in the first place. The only thing he asks is for you to do a *kneeling for forgiveness* at a church service when you are ready. Ask for mercy regarding your fondness of drink."

Wayne sat silently looking at the floor. He finally looked up and directed his vision to his brother and said, "I will do this to bring our families back together. I have missed so much. I have missed you, Levi. The death of our parents..."

"*Nee,* do not go there. We will be happy again, Wayne. Just look at your family. You can become stronger for them."

Wayne nodded. "I will find work and a place to live as soon as I can."

"I have thoughts regarding this, as well. We could fix up our family home for you and your family. Also, you know I am not a farmer. I love my horses. Why not you take over all the farming and I'll work the south portion of the land, where I grow feed for the animals? This land will support us both."

Wayne did not say a word for a moment, but Anna gasped at Levi's solution. Her husband shook his head at her in a silent way to communicate for her to be still.

Finally, he questioned, "You would do this for us?"

Levi nodded. "You are my brother, and I love you. You are welcome here."

On that word, they fell into silence as they ate. Even the *boppli* slept through the meal.

Miriam was at a loss as to what to say to Wayne and Anna. They were strangers to her. If truth is known, Wayne was as much a stranger to Levi. They had not seen each other for over ten years. The older man had to be at least forty years old.

"You are welcome here from me as well. I would love to help you with the *boppli*."

When she had first met Anna for her appointment, she never realized the age difference between the couple. Twenty years was a lot. She'd have to ask Levi just how old his brother was. He looked old but living the way they did probably took a toll on him. With good food and a warm, safe place to live, surely both he and Anna's future health might return.

The babies were healthy, but how much had they stripped from their mothers', bones, teeth, and general health?

"Miriam?"

Levi's voice pulled her from her thoughts. "Sorry. I guess I am too tired to sit here any longer." She managed to eat half a biscuit with honey and some of her meal, pushing much of it around on her plate. "I'm not very hungry, but it was delicious, Anna. Thank you for doing this."

"Run off to bed. We can handle everything here. I'll see you in the morning at breakfast after I feed the horses, and with my brother's help," he smiled at Wayne showing his joking manner, "the chores should go fast. I have no plans tomorrow but to get this family settled in with us."

Miriam squeezed his hand and said goodnight to her new family and left the room.

It took all her energy just to slip into her long cotton nightgown and drop into bed. Her eyes closed as her head touched the pillow.

CHAPTER 6

The days flew by, with Miriam becoming more comfortable having the extra family members at their home. Anna was happy and joyful. She laughed all the time and found funny attributes in any situation. With the twins in the house, they created a lot to laugh about as well.

The day approached where the women of the district gathered together to quilt. Or that is how it started. As newer girls were married, some of them preferred knitting or crocheting over the quilting. These women sat in the room, working on their projects, and they all talked in a flurry of words.

Following breakfast, Miriam asked Anna, "Would you like to join me tomorrow at the women's circle?"

Anna, having nursed one baby and got her to sleep, was now nursing the other. Then she would place her by her sister in a playpen Wayne and Levi had picked up at an auction. What a great invention this item was. It gave the girls the freedom to lay together and explore their surroundings. They were too little to do much but look at each other, but a time would come when safety was necessary.

"I have not learned to quilt." Anna looked at the floor, and a red blush rose from her neck to her face. "My family had no money for anything more than food for all ten of us children. We had love from maem, but *daed,* he was no provider. He drank."

Miriam was not sure she wanted to hear this story, but she reached over and squeezed Anna's hand in reassurance. "You do not have to tell me this if you do not want to."

Anna shook her head. "*Nee,* I do. You see, I wanted out of poverty and the shame of having our district provide for us. When rumspringa came, I went into town and took a job as a waitress. I had a friend who worked there, and she let me stay with her. It helped us both with expenses."

"You were a brave girl, Anna. I would not have the courage to be on my own."

"I was so scared my *Daed* might make me come home, but he did not. He even frequented the cafe, but he never spoke to me. Of course, he was always drunk, but in some small way, I felt he did me a favor. By not acknowledging me, he saved me the embarrassment of everyone knowing I was his daughter."

Miriam nodded. "Your life could not have been easy."

"Do not get me wrong, I miss them so much, especially my maem. I would love to show maem my *boppli.*"

"Maybe one day we can figure out how to help you do this."

Anna smiled with trembling lips. "I pray so," she whispered.

"So do you want to go with me? I am sure one of the ladies there will take you under their wing. We do more than quilting. I crochet, not well yet, but I am trying. Some knit, some sew or embroidered. Maybe you can find something you wish to do, and I'm sure the women will help you learn."

Anna stood to place the *boppli* in the playpen with her sister. "I would like that very much. Thank *Gott* I have you, Miriam."

Miriam's heart swelled as she watched the girl walk from the room.

Miriam carried one of the *boppli* while Anna carried the other. The little ones were growing fast. Anna handed the *boppli* to Miriam and Miriam watched Anna gracefully get into the family buggy and reached over for her little ones. It was a good thing they were only going to the

Eischler's house as it was only a couple miles. Holding both *boppli* got heavy.

Pulling herself up into the buggy, Miriam took the reins and started the horses on their journey.

Within thirty minutes, they arrived at their destination. Miriam stifled a laugh when she spotted faces at the windows and through the screen door. Seems Miriam and Anna were the entertainment for the day.

She could imagine the chatter about Levi's brother's family staying with them. The circle always filled with gossip. The ladies enjoyed the socialization, but sometimes it became too much for Miriam to handle. And of course, they were still trying to get her to tell them about her patients. She refused to do so. Her *Mammi* taught her never to divulge a patient's' information. Shaking her head, she knew how these rumors went. They flew around the community, and the story changed from one person to another. *Nee,* it was better to protect her patients.

"Are you ready for this, Anna?" Miriam asked.

Anna handed her Abby. She could only tell because she had on pink nail polish. It was unusual for Amish, but in this instance, it helped keep the babies apart. Their father laughed about the situation and told the family Emma might soon become jealous, and require her own unique color.

The young woman quickly rounded the buggy and took both her *boppli* from Miriam to allow her to jump down from the seat.

"I'll grab the diaper bag for you," Miriam spoke, turned around to grab the bag. Once she gathered everything, she hopped down, and the two women made their way to Bishop Eischler's house.

Mrs. Eischler and her daughter, Mary, made a safe spot to lay the *boppli* on a large bed near the living room where the circle was being held. They put pillows around the girls and made sure they could not fall off if one of them took a notion to roll. Of course, neither of them had the ability yet, but it was coming.

Mary offered to look in on the little ones frequently so Anna could join in the festivities.

Anna sat beside Miriam on the sofa and watched her hands work the yarn. "I don't think I could ever have the patience to count all the loops."

"Truly, it is not difficult. If it were, I would not be able to do it."

Anna sat there a while longer, then stood. "I think I will go see how to quilt. It looks so beautiful."

"It is a beautiful pattern, a Wedding Ring quilt which Mary's mother is making for her hope chest."

"Will she marry soon?" Anna asked.

"Maybe, but it is the way of the district to keep courting a secret. The community is not told until the marriage is announced in the fall at a church service."

"Oh."

"Is this the way your district was as well?" Miriam frowned. She wondered about Anna and her district.

Anna offered no answer and walked away to join the others at the quilt.

The *boppli* remained sleeping for most of the afternoon.

CHAPTER 7

Daylight drew shorter and shorter as the fall season became colder. Miriam dreaded the long nights. It felt so claustrophobic as if the world was closing in on her. She still did all the same things, but everything took longer.

The flag on the mailbox was up, indicating the mail had arrived. Also, Levi had not brought it in yet. Instead of taking the shorter way to the house, she trudged to the mailbox. Pulling out envelopes which looked like ads, she found a folded piece of yellow, lined paper, and she unfolded it and read.

Wayne
Keep your mouth shut!
We are watching your every move.
If not, your wife and kids will regret it!

A chill ran through Miriam's body, and she reached for her healing bag. What in the world was this about?

Something about Levi's brother made her uneasy. She was not sure what caused her to feel this way, but in any case, that was the way she felt.

Miriam nearly ran into the house, but only Anna was there. She heard her singing to the babies as she took the steps to the second floor in a hurry. She had to find out where Levi was, and the quickest way was to speak to Anna. Miriam stuffed the note in her coat pocket. No way would she show her new sister-in-law.

Standing in the doorway to the *boppli's* room, Miriam took in the beautiful scene with the younger woman rocking both little ones in her arms. "Anna," she whispered just loud enough to get the girl's attention. "Can you tell me where to find Levi? I need to speak to him right away."

"I'm not sure. I heard Levi and Wayne leave with our buckboard about an hour ago."

Miriam nodded and raised her finger to her lips, indicating she would be quiet and turned away from the room. Rushing back down the stairs, she put her coat on a hook in the mudroom then went into the kitchen. There was *kaffe* on the stove, and she poured herself a cup then took it to the table. She had to calm down. Her heart was beating at an unhealthy pace.

Why was someone threatening Wayne and his family? What was it about? Miriam was not familiar with these people so she could not come up with any thoughts about it. Her husband didn't even know his brother after so many years apart. Did she want these people sharing her home? Did it place she and Levi in danger as well?

Ach, she wished Levi were here to talk to. She realized her thoughts were growing larger and larger, and her fear swamped her. Taking a calming breath, she looked around the kitchen. A pleasant aroma of something cooking came from the oven.

It was past five o'clock.

Anna walked into the room. "I think the little ones will sleep for a while. What a fuss they put up all day. Nothing I tried pleased them."

"*Jah*, they are a month old now. They are probably getting bored."

"Bored? At that age?" Anna was aghast.

Miriam nodded. "Have you been playing with them?"

Anna's eyes grew wide in surprise. She shook her head. "*Nee*, just taking care of them."

"Tomorrow I will be here. Ruby works the busy weekend day. I think she's bored as well." Miriam laughed. "Now her son Matthew and his wife Hannah are running the farm stay, Ruby has little to do." Changing thoughts from the note calmed her. "We can play with Abby and Emma to see if it will help them. If not, I have a calming elixir I made. It is on my shelves in the basement."

Anna's eyes grew wide. "What are you talking about? I understand you are a midwife but are you a doctor as well?"

Miriam shook her head. "No, I'm the local healer. I use herbs I grow in my garden in the summer, blend them into a potion that helps people. I'm sorry to frighten you."

"You scared me to death, Miriam. I thought you were a witch or something."

Miriam smiled at the young woman. "No. I was trained by my grandmother to heal and help people."

Anna opened the oven and took out a roaster. Meatloaf, surrounded by baking potatoes and carrots filled it. "I did not have much time today, so I just threw this together."

Miriam sniffed the air. "It smells great. What a fantastic way to cook. Do it all at once."

"*Jah*, my *mamm* showed me several tricks for busy days. I guess you could say I was trained in the art of frugal cooking." She laughed at her comparison between her and Miriam.

"Where do your parents live?" Miriam asked. She didn't want to pry, but she wanted to know the girl better.

"Ohio."

"This is a ways from here. How in the world did you meet Wayne?"

Anna pushed the roaster pan back into the oven, tossed the potholders onto the counter then went to sit across from Miriam. "Wayne came to Lindville, which is not far from Pennsylvania, with my brother James. Our surname is Hooley. They both had jobs at a factory in Pittsburg which closed. Wayne came with James to our home, but I had seen him at the cafe where I worked a few times."

"I had no idea. Well, really, I do not know your husband at all. I hope to remedy this."

Anna smiled at her. "I am sure you will hit it off with him. He is quite a bit like Levi."

"So he arrived, and you fell in love just like a fairytale."

Anna shook her head, and the corners of her mouth drooped down. "Not really. *Jah,* we fell in love, but it was not a pretty story. You see my father is a bad drunk, I think I told you before, but my brother does not fall far from the tree."

"*Ach,* I am so sorry, Anna. I shouldn't have asked."

"*Nee,* do not feel this way. I want you to know how good a man Wayne is. When my father and James were arrested for thefts of farm implements, Wayne got me out of there. We got married in a civil ceremony on the same day."

"What a story," Miriam cried. "And you came back here?"

Anna nodded. "We actually came to this district, and Wayne spoke to Bishop Yoder. We wanted to return to my husband's home, but the leader would not let us. Our only recourse was to find somewhere cheap to live. Wayne found odd jobs to keep us afloat."

Miriam shook her head. Had Bishop Yoder hurt everyone in the district? "You know, we found out that the shunning was not an authorized action. Wayne is free to live in the district with no recourse."

"*Jah,* we know and want to spend our lives here. I am so glad to be out of my life in Ohio. I miss my *maem* and two older sisters. But they are both married and have children. The last I heard, *maem,* lived with my oldest sister and helped take care of her children and home."

"So what happened with your *daed* and brother?"

"*Daed* was sentenced to five years in prison and my brother only one year. He just helped once, and the authorities did not have as much information to sentence him longer. I heard he was out of prison and trying to get money from maem."

"I hope she has not given him any!" Miriam slapped her hand across her mouth. "I'm sorry! I should not have said that."

Anna laughed loudly, then forced herself to be quite so not to wake up the *boppli*. "It is ok, Miriam. I feel the same way. Oh, Miriam, I nearly forgot to tell you! A man stopped by a while ago. He was looking for you. His wife is having pains, but he said she still had a month to go."

Miriam shook her head in wonder. "Was the man short and round with bright red hair?"

"*Jah,* He was."

Laughing Miriam told her sister-in-law, "Probably Homer Hansen. He and his wife are young and terrified of everything to do with this baby, their first." She poured a cup of *kaffe* then sat at the table. "I'm sure Letty is having early pains, her body's way of preparing for the birth."

"I remember those. I thought having pains were so bad at the time. How silly I was. When the real pain came, I could easily tell the difference." The girl smiled, remembering the birth of her daughters. "Why not lay down and take a nap before supper? What if she is right? You need your rest. You work too hard, Miriam."

"I hate to leave you with the *boppli* and all the meal preparation. Are you sure there is nothing I can help you with?"

Anna shook her head. "Nothing. You just go rest."

Miriam walked from her kitchen and went to the bedroom. The note in her pocket seemed to burn a hole into her leg. She would tell Levi about it later. She so wanted all this to work out, but the tone of the note frightened her.

Miriam jerked her head to the side and swiped her hand across her lips. She didn't want to wake up. Her body relaxed back into sleep when the sensation against her lips happened again. Her eyes popped open. Levi sat beside her moving the ends of her hair against her lips.

"Hi," she said softly. Pulling herself into a sitting position, she leaned forward and kissed her husband softly on his lips. "I am sorry to be so tired, but with Anna handling the kitchen, I took advantage of her."

Levi kissed her back. "I am happy you did. With the family arriving, and you delivering all these *boppli*, you have overworked yourself."

"*Jah*, I have, but it makes good news. There are only two *boppli* left to birth on my calendar. We might get a break." Miriam smiled brightly. She felt better and more rested than she had for a long time. "I wanted to ask you something. What would you think if I quit working at the store?"

He reached out for her hand and pulled her up to stand in front of him. He smiled at her.

"I have no problem with it at all, the person you should be asking is your sister, Ruby."

Miriam nodded, deep in thought at his decision. She'd been afraid to bring it up with Ruby, but recently, Ruby had been at loose ends. She even told Miriam how lost she felt now Matthew and Hannah had taken over the farm stay. The only time Ruby worked was when the house was full, and Hannah needed her assistance with the cooking for a large group.

"Ruby does not have anything to do. This would benefit her, as well as me." Miriam brushed through her hip length hair and quickly swirled it into a bun at the back of her head. In a couple of movements, she had the bobby pins in, and she was attaching her *Kapp* with them as well. "I may talk to her tomorrow. That is why I wanted your feelings on this before I brought it up to her."

"We don't need the percentage of the money you get from your sales at the store. It would help your sister more if she did not have to share with you." Levi squeezed her shoulders, then spoke, "I'll let you get straightened out and meet you in the kitchen?"

Miriam shook her head. "*Nee*, I have something serious to talk to you about. I found this in the mail today. I do not understand what to think of it, and it frightens me." She reached in her dress pocket and pulled out the note and handed it to Levi.

Levi looked at her quizzically then began to read it. Miriam watched his face pale then turn red in anger. "I will speak to my brother. Now! We cannot have him involved in something which would surely get us all under the *bann*. I will not hear of it. I will have him out of here tonight if he does not tell me what is going on."

"*Ach*, Levi!" Miriam cried. "You cannot do this. What about the *boppli* and Anna? They would not have anywhere to go."

"I will let the girl and babies stay, but my brother will be out in the cold."

He tossed open the door and stomped out, closing the bedroom door with more force than Miriam had ever seen. She knew her husband had a temper, but the short bursts she had seen were nothing like this. She was afraid for Wayne.

Please Gott, let the two brothers come to some sort of understanding. She whispered her prayer aloud. She took all her problems to *Gott*, and each morning she thanked him for giving her another day of life. Miriam opened the bedroom door and heard Levi holler, "Wayne! Put down the *boppli* and meet me in the barn!"

Miriam cringed. She knew she had to go out to the kitchen and see Anna, but what would she say to her? Taking a deep breath, she hurried to her new sister-in-law.

Levi sat down on a hay bale and pointed at the one in front of him for Wayne. He shook his head. What was Wayne involved with? The way the family was living, it did not show he was making money at anything illegal. But what?

"Brother! What is the matter?" Wayne rushed to ask and stood in front of Levi. He finally sat when Levi pointed to the bale of hay again.

Levi pulled the note from his coat and handed it to Wayne. "You tell me what the problem is."

Wayne read the note. He raised his eyes and looked directly into Levi's. "I cannot tell you."

"Are you prepared to leave my farm? This is what will happen if you do not tell me what this is all about."

Wayne shook his head.

Levi felt a bit sorry for his brother, but he could not have him keeping secrets from him. It was not safe for his family nor Wayne's. "Is it serious? Dangerous?"

Wayne finally nodded but did not utter a word.

"You had better speak up. I am serious." Levi crossed his arms over his chest, not backing down on his demand.

Finally, Wayne caved and faced his brother. "About a month ago, I was out hunting and came across a meeting of five men at an old run-down barn." Levi nodded in encouragement for Wayne to continue.

"They were talking about rustling horses. Expensive horses and selling them."

"You did not tell the authorities I suspect."

"*Nee.* I could not do so. They would have arrested me."

Levi shook his head, not understanding. "Why?"

"Because!" Wayne hollered. "Because it was at night. I was poaching deer for us to eat. I could not go to jail and leave Anna alone with the *boppli*." Wayne stood and in agitation paced back and forth on the packed dirt floor. "Besides, I do not know the names of those men. They might think I do, but I do not!"

His brother's words sounded like he was a ten-year-old caught shoplifting. "Why are you so afraid?"

"Because those men know where I am apparently, and they must think I was near enough to hear them during their conversation. If they see the police here, they will do something. I have to get out of here."

Levi shook his head. "Nee brother. You cannot run. You acted this way when you were younger when bishop Yoder shunned you. You were not even baptized. You see how well that worked out."

"What am I going to do?"
"We will figure this out together and resolve the danger."

CHAPTER 8

Levi heard the buggy coming up the drive. He patted the horse's neck and stopped his brushing. "Best to see who comes visiting, Mayhem."

He made his way through the barn door, trying not to lose any heat. Upon seeing the Bishop driving up, Levi pushed the wide barn doors open so the man could drive the buggy into the warm barn.

Once Bishop Eischler settled the buggy Levi hitched the horse and gave him feed and water. "What brings thee out this way, Bishop? Do I need to find Wayne?"

"*Nee*, Levi. I come to speak to you about troubles around the district."

Levi must have looked as bewildered as he felt. "Come, Bishop, let's sit and tell me what has happened."

The Bishop sat across from Levi and started, "Your mentor Mr. Schmidt has had a couple of mares stolen. The thieves took them from the barn at night and proceeded to load them into a waiting trailer in the field."

The Bishop took a breath as Levi rose in agitation from his seat over the news. "Does he know who did this?"

"*Nee* Levi, he needs help and asked for you. On a sad note, one of the mares dropped her foal in the field."

Levi moaned over this announcement. He knew all the horses at Mr. Schmidt's and especially the mares.

"He did find the foal, and with *Gott's* help, it should survive."

"Good, were there any clues?"

"*Nee,* nothing."

Levi slowly took his seat. "Have any other farms had problems?"

"One other, the Kelso brothers. They took three from them, two mares and one stud. They actually used two trailers."

"Sounds as though they are well planned. Might be we should contact Asher..." He didn't have time to finish his statement before the Bishop halted him.

"We will handle this in our way."

"*Jah*, of course."

Levi knew many of the older members in the district were still mulling about the police involvement over the missing girls a few months ago, which resulted in murders. He kept his own feelings to himself and would *nee* say otherwise.

"I will go right over to Mr. Schmidt and then the Kelso farm. Bishop, we may need to call a council of the breeders."

"Yes, I have sent out the call. We will meet on Wednesday, two days should give you time. They will want to go over what you find and what measures we need to take."

His hand moved over his pants to brush the hay away and realized the threatening note to Wayne was there. *Nee*, he did not dare show the message to the bishop. The man would feel as Levi had at first. He would assume Wayne was involved.

"I will saddle up as it will be quicker for me to ride through the fields."

"*Jah*, you are right, of course."

Levi backed the Bishop's buggy out of the barn. Little else was said.

Once mounted, Levi looked down at Wayne, "Take care of them and keep our home safe, Wayne."

"Yes, brother."

"I am going to ride over to the store and tell Miriam what has happened."

Anna moved up to the horse, preventing Levi from leaving, "Yes, Anna?" Levi was a little surprised by her actions as she usually appeared too meek to speak.

"You should be careful, my brother. We will keep our combined family and the horses safe."

He tipped his hat to her and smiled. It warmed his heart that she was feeling closer to him as a new family member. Something in her warning bothered him a bit, but he could not pinpoint what it was. He supposed the situation was getting on his nerves. The horse must have felt his anxiousness and took off at a fast clip over the road.

The store was in the same direction he would take to get to the other farms. He would not go without stopping and telling Miriam.

"There it is, come on, let's go see my wife," Levi said to his horse.

Before he made it to the door, Miriam stood on the small covered porch looking so beautiful. He could see the questions in her eyes for his unexpected visit.

"Hello."

She giggled at him. "Hello, husband."

He swung his leg over the horse and righted himself. Standing there, he stood looking at her. He loved her so much. Their problems were sorting themselves out, and they had become much happier.

"Why have you stopped, Levi?"

"I know I've been a stranger around here..."

"Could be I will be home, so you won't have to race over." Miriam's soft laughter sounded like spring in the bitter cold.

"Please, lovely, let's go inside for a bit as I must be going soon."

He held the door for her, taking in the soft fragrance unique to Miriam.

Regretfully, he told her of the Bishop's visit and where he would be going. All humor left her pretty face. "I will be careful. Is Wayne involved in this? Is this what the note was about?"

Levi did not want to bring her into this, but there was no other way. "Yes. He overhead the talk of rustling, but he could not tell who the men were. He had only seen one or two but was not involved with them. They are from his old location. I guess they feel it is easier to steal than to work for a living."

Levi pulled Miriam into his arms to hold her and kissed her forehead. "This afternoon, come home as soon as possible, Miriam. Anna will be beating the bushes if you don't."

"Does Anna know about all of this?"

"She does now. Wayne told her."

Taking her shoulders, he placed her to one side so he could reach the door. "I'll be home as soon as I can, but there are some people I need to talk to. We have to work out some sort of plan, but I have no clue what it is."

Levi walked through the doorway without looking back. It always saddened him to leave Miriam.

CHAPTER 9

Miriam drove her enclosed buggy home through the deep, blowing snow. The wiper blades whipped across the window she hoped the battery kept operating as it also powered the front and the back lighting systems. She and her *Mammi* purchased the buggy for the healing and birthing business a few years back, and it still looked like a new carriage.

The closer to home she got, the more her eyes wanted to drift shut. She had been busy this week with two births, and tonight she'd been over to Elmer Eckhardt's place. His wife Lucy fell down the cement basement stairs and severely wrenched her back. She was not a young woman, more middle-aged and Miriam knew an injury could have life-long effects.

Elmer had called her from the neighbor's phone shanty as they were getting ready for supper. Levi had not been happy with her, but re-alizing the Eckhardt's place was so close, he relaxed about her traveling there and knowing this was not a birth helped.

Miriam had completed a hands-on energy healing, and when she left the couples home, the woman felt much better.

Being the powwow healer in their district was difficult. Some people lived by her healings and folk remedies, but others? *Nee*, they were uncomfortable and her worst enemy Rebecca Zohn, had called her a witch once when she was talking to a group of younger women after a singing. Mammi told her the girl was jealous, and she had to ignore the negative comments.

Miriam sighed when she saw the lights of her home through the blowing snow. Guiding the horse into the turn on the path leading to the house, fatigue swamped her.

She drove past the house and toward the barn. Levi was waiting. He opened the barn door for her to drive in. All was well with her life.

Miriam sat on the single seat that went from one side to the other of the buggy, too tired to move. Something had to give in her life. Between working at the store daily and the midwifery and healings, she couldn't keep up. Never in her life had she been this tired.

Suddenly, the buggy door opened, and Levi reached in and helped her out. Sweeping her into his arms, he cradled her in his warmth and filled her with love.

"I'm glad you are back so soon. How is Mrs. Eckhardt?"

Miriam turned in his arms and stepped toward the buggy to retrieve her medical supply bag. She needed to refill a few herbs she used during the healing. "The woman will be alright. Probably a bit sore, but nothing was broken, and she had no lacerations. These longer dresses and heavy socks are protection at times."

Levi laughed at her observance. He was walking the horse to a stall. "Go in and have your supper while I brush down Buster. You must be starving."

"*Nee*, I think I'm too tired to feel hunger."

"At least try to eat, it is not healthy to go so long between meals." Levi offered.

Miriam opened the barn door wide enough to slip through and turned, saying, "I'll try to eat something for you. I'll see you at the house."

The next morning at eight a.m. Miriam turned the stores closed sign to the open side. The store would be quiet for a couple hours, and it gave her time to deal with the previous days' receipts and to straighten the displays.

She trudged around, sighing each time she found items in the wrong place. The customers picked things up, then when they found something they liked, even more, they dropped what was in their hands and replaced it with the new item.

The smell of the *kaffe* brewing made her stomach lurch. She knew she had been too tired to eat much last night, but Levi had come in the house and had sat with her while he encouraged her to eat the last bit of rice pudding. It was just too heavy for her, and now she was paying for it.

She and her husband had talked about her quitting the store. She felt sure Levi thought she would never do it. She wondered if she could leave. It was more than a job to her.

"*Gute mariye.*" Her sister, Ruby, breezed into the room and removed her coat and scarf, placing them on the pegs by the door. "Goodness, Miriam, you look unwell."

"Tired is all. I have had a lot going on the past few days. Two births and one healing."

Ruby pulled out a chair, and the two women sat behind the wall which separated the store from the business area. "You know you can count on me to help out when you need to go. Or you can stay home and rest if you have a night away."

Reaching out, Miriam took Ruby's hand. Ruby was so kind to her. It broke her heart to continue on in this vein of conversation, but she just had to. "I know, but I've always been reluctant. You are busy with the farm stay and making sure Matthew and Hannah have a firm grasp of running the business."

Ruby shook her head. "*Nee*, not anymore. They are doing fine. If only Hannah could learn to bake. It will take time. Until then, they will have to rely on the bakery in town. That is if old mister Hamlin can continue. I've heard talk he wants to sell the bakery."

"He must be getting up in age, goodness, we used to go there to get a free cookie when we were young. We couldn't have been any older than eight or nine."

"Yes, feels like yesterday. I will say Carly loves to bake and is constantly filling the pantry with goodies for the guests and bread every day. Hannah would sorely miss our friend."

Miriam agreed, "I love her muffins, they are a meal in themselves, and I can't wait to see what her flavor is today."

"The house smelled marvelous this morning, all the sweet baking aroma flows right over to the *dawdi haus*." Ruby couldn't help but laugh over their enjoyment of Carly's creations.

"So what are you doing with your time, Ruby?"

"Not much. I'm bored to tears sitting in the *dawdi haus* watching it snow."

Miriam stood and stepped into the doorway to see if customers were coming up the road. No one. Maybe this was the time to talk to her sister about her thoughts.

"Ruby? Um...I need to, well..."

Ruby's eyes narrowed as she looked at her. "What is it sister, you appear afraid to talk to me. What is wrong?"

"Nothing is wrong." Miriam was having a hard time with this decision. She looked down at the floor and could not cast Ruby a glance. "I want to quit working here at the store. I have so much to do with the birthing *boppli* and trying to keep up the house. Levi needs more of my time. And his brother, wife and two *boppli* are living with us until the men can get the old farmhouse into shape for them to move over there. I feel as if I'm losing control of everything, including my mind!"

Ruby stood and took Miriam into her arms. "There, there, sister. I understand. Here, sit down with me and we will talk about this."

Tears rolled down Miriam's cheeks, and she pulled a snow white hankie from her apron pocket and dabbed at the moisture. "I did not know how to tell you this. I feel so bad for saying it." Another round of tears fell from her eyes.

"Nonsense, I have nothing better to do with my time, and I would enjoy taking on the store. We have always worked closely on it, so I do not need training," Ruby laughed, which caused Miriam to smile with her.

"So when do you want to begin this change? I'm so worn out I could walk out of here today and dump it all in your lap."

"So go home. Do not worry your sweet soul about me, sister. I truly will enjoy having something to do with my time. "

Miriam began gathering her things just as Levi opened the store door and the bells rang, a notification Miriam used to notify her she had a customer. "Levi, what are you doing here at this time of day?"

He wiped his snow-covered boots on the rug by the door then walked through the store, heading for his wife. "I'm going into town and visit the livestock sales barn." Pouring himself a cup of *kaffe*. Levi blew on the hot liquid before taking a small sip. "I'm buying a new stud standard-breed. I'm hoping he will solve our problems."

"I can see where this is heading, Levi." Miriam stood in front of him, wringing her hands. "Please do not do this."

Miriam watched Levi's frown. He did not like her to interfere. He told her about the missing horses a few weeks ago.

"It is the only way. Asher thinks..."

"Asher?" The name came out louder and sharper than she intended. She was surprised he had even contacted Asher, the chief of police in the area. Levi told her the bishop wanted it handled by their community. He could be stern in his words, but she knew it was just his concern showing. He had a deep-seated love for his community. This was one of the things which drew her to him, and she loved him so. "Why did you bring the police into it when you were told by the bishop to let the community handle it?"

"This is bigger and more dangerous than we can handle, Miriam. I took Asher into my confidence. He will let us handle it, but we can contact him if something goes wrong."

"He would do that?"

"He said he will, and I trust him, He's Amish. He understands us.

"Oh, on another subject, I did as you asked." He pulled a cell phone from his pocket. Miriam smiled and hugged him tightly.

"I am glad you approve. Asher is a good man. He will keep your news under his hat if he said he will," Ruby said.

"Okay, enough of this horse talk. I hear about the horses' day and night. Should I tell him, Ruby?" Miriam finished putting Levi's phone number in her phone and hers in his then turned toward her sister.

Ruby laughed. "You might as well, he will find out about it soon enough."

Levi rushed toward her, grasped her waist and twirled her around, causing her dress to spin around her in the air. "You're finally going to tell me about our own *boppli*? Wonderful. I am so excited to be a father!"

Miriam righted herself and stood in silence, staring at him. "What are you talking about, Levi?" Why did he think her news had to do with a *boppli*? Surely, he did not know she was with child. She would know such a thing, after all, she was a midwife. Then thoughts of nausea, fatigue, and fainting struck her. *Nee*. She could not be, could she?

She just stood in the middle of the room with both Levi and Ruby staring at her. Suddenly, they all began laughing. "I-I think I might be. With my heavy workload the past few weeks, I thought I was overworked."

"You have been, Miriam. Why not tell Levi what we really talked about earlier?"

Levi gave Miriam a one-armed hug and said, "Since I let the cat out of the bag about the *boppli*, maybe you better tell me what is really going on."

"Go ahead, sister tell him our plans."

Taking a deep breath, Miriam began, "I am quitting working here at the store. I have so much more to do with the midwifery, and now Wayne, Anna, and the children. I want to be home to support you emotionally, and if you have chores for me, like driving to town to pick up supplies, you may need."

Levi's eyes grew wide in surprise. "That...that is wonderful. I'm just surprised you really are doing this. With the *boppli* coming, it is perfect timing. Apparently, you agree, Ruby."

"Oh, yes! I have been so bored with nothing to do around the farm stay now Matthew and Hannah have taken over. This will be perfect for me."

Levi smiled at Ruby then at Miriam. "I suppose this is all working out for everyone."

"It is, and now my husband," Miriam gave Levi a playful grin which made her eyes sparkle. "told me, a trained midwife, that I am with child, I need to be home even more. I have baby clothes to make."

"Or you could buy some from your sister." Levi picked up a blue one-piece covering and ran his fingers over the soft material.

"Miriam, run along home," Ruby said, "It's starting to snow harder, and the wind has picked up.

"I rode my horse, so I cannot take you home, but I will make the horse purchase quickly."

Miriam slipped into her wool coat, tied on her black hat over her *Kapp*, then wrapped the long wool scarf around her neck. "I will be on my way then."

Levi opened the door for her, once again setting off the bells.

"Be safe, both of you," Ruby called out to them as they left the store.

CHAPTER 10

Ruby had taken over the store full-time for nearly two weeks. She plunked down in the soft desk chair behind the short wall, hidden somewhat from customers. Today everyone arrived at the same time and left this way as well. At once. Not that there were too many customers.

She took a bottle of cold water from the barrel near the check out station before she came back here for her break. Twisting off the lid, she tipped back the bottle and took a long drink. Even though winter barely arrived, the store was hot when the stove heating the area was recently stoked.

Closing her eyes for a moment helped clear her mind. She worried about her sister Miriam. Pregnant, busy with birthing babies and healings, and now, all these shunned families coming to their property to live. She admired her sister, but she still worried. What more could happen in their district? Last spring had been the kidnappings and the murder of the teacher; this winter, horse thieves, and the new families.

The farm stay was forgotten in the gossip mill with all that transpired over the last few weeks. Now she was the only one working at the store, she was occupied most of the day. Closing the store a couple of days a week crossed her mind, and with winter coming, the sales dropped to minimal amounts. Really it was not worth opening even one day.

The ringing of the bell over the door snapped her from her reverie. In walked David Fisher. Ruby's heart felt as if it had jumped to her throat. Something about this man made her breathing difficult and her breath to catch.

"*Welkom,* David. What brings you in on this cold, snowy day?"

"You do."

"Me?"

"*Jah.*" He reached behind him for the doorknob then turned and went out onto the covered porch. When he stepped back in, he had an ornately carved and finished clock in his arms. "This is for you as thanks for all you did for my family to make Hannah's wedding so nice."

Ruby could not fathom what to say. Never had she received such a gorgeous gift for herself. "I'm stunned, David. All I can say is thank you."

He walked around the divider wall and placed the large clock onto the counter. Looking Ruby directly in the eyes he asked, "mind if I sit a spell?"

"*Nee,* do sit a spell." She pushed the other rolling chair toward him. "Nothing much is going on here. Winter is taking over a bit early. I would not be surprised to have a white Christmas. I have been sitting here wondering if I should just close up until spring."

"And not have sales for the Englisch Christmas shoppers?"

"*Ach,* I have a plan for this." Ruby bit at her lower lip and looked away from David. He caused her heart to gallop and her breathing ragged. Could she tell him what she had been up to during her long evenings? She took a calming breath and looked back toward the man. He had a cute grin pulling at his full lips.

"And your plan is?" He looked around the room to assure there were no customers before he said, "So do not worry about what you have been up to. I see you are truly a *gut* Amish woman, but a little more progressive than tradition...as am I. Do tell me."

His words relaxed her worries. She blew out the end of her anxiety with a sigh, and told him, "I have been taking pictures of all the store items with my cell phone. At night when our children are asleep upstairs, I have been updating the farm stay website with pages of the store and listing items for sale." She opened her arms, indicating the whole store.

David's mouth dropped open, and his blue eyes grew wide.

Ruby swallowed with difficulty. *Oh nee, she had done it now!* If only she could take back her words! Ruby had always been in trouble with her husband. She was the one with the idea of gas generators for the electric refrigerator and freezer in the basement. Then it was the electric washer and electric lights. *Ach,* the tiffs they had over buying those items. He finally gave in to all her demands, but he insisted the generators go in a shed he built close to the back porch. The old bishop had never found out.

This did not stop her husband from thinking she was too Englisch. Maybe she was, but she trusted *Gott* and her Anabaptist religion as well as loved her community and all the members of it.

Now they had a new bishop, Matthew spoke to him about getting direct electric lines to the house. The man agreed. It completely surprised both Ruby and Matthew when the bishop decided in their favor. The farm stay contributed a lot of money to the fund, which helped pay medical bills for people in the district, build barns after catastrophes and on and on. The bishop needed all the businesses to thrive for the security of the community.

"I imagine you feel I should be shunned."

David burst out laughing, splitting the tension in the room. "Oh Ruby, you are one of a kind. Of course, I do not think you should be shunned. You are a lovely, proper Amish woman doing what's best for your family. You are a true entrepreneur."

"But if the bishop found out…"

"And why should he care at all? He knows about the computer and the farm stay website. The store is just one more element of it."

"True. I must be overthinking it."

David stood to leave. "What will you do with your time if you close the store?"

Ruby shrugged. "I am not sure. Without the farm, I do not have much to do.

"I have a question for you," David said. He ran a tan finger over the wood countertop following the grain as he deliberated his words. "You see, my business is growing fast. With all my new employees I have arriving, there will be a tremendous amount of paperwork. Then there are all the documents for my purchases of seed, fencing for my new property, all sorts of things I will need in the spring."

"How many workers are you taking on?"

"At least three of the five that are coming this week." he ran out of steam and sat back down.

Ruby followed suit. She could see the man needed someone to talk too. "What a massive amount of work you have to do."

"I can do all of this, but I have a problem with record keeping." He shook his head. "You should see my desk. Piles of bills and receipts. I was wondering if you could help me out?"

Ruby didn't answer for a bit. What was he asking of her? "I am not sure, David. What can I do?"

"You did all the books for the farm stay, *jah?*"

She nodded. Now she knew what David wanted, but she might have to divulge another secret. When would all her skeletons in the cupboard come out? And here she was giving them away to the only man who had created turmoil in her heart since losing her husband.

Oh well, he knew about the website so what? She closed her eyes and opened her mouth, and with it, she released a bit of the hold she had on her own heart. "David, you are my friend, so I'm going to trust you with this secret as well. I do the books on the computer." She placed her head on her arms, which she had crossed on the counter.

"Hey, don't despair. It is OK. But I want to know... how did you learn all of this? I am truly impressed with your knowledge."

"You are?"

"*Jah*, I am."

She raised her head, and tears ran down her cheeks. "I do not know how to do paper versions of books. I'm sorry I will not be a help to you."

David took her small hands into his rough, work-worn hands. How about I talk to the Bishop about my need for a computer? Then you could use mine. Do you remember the small room at the front of the house near the living area?

She nodded.

"I have made it into my office. We could set up the computer there, and you could come and go by the front door."

Ruby mulled over the idea. There was no good reason not to do this for him, although she worried about spending so much time with him. Over the months she knew him, she began to fall in love with him?

Since Hannah had been found, she returned to help her family with meals and housework. Ruby had been helping at the Fisher home while Hannah was missing, but now, she saw David only when they were helping arrange the wedding. "*Awk,* I forgot to tell you Mrs. Guthrie will be here as well."

His words pulled her from the thoughts,

"She will keep our house and cook for us. Her room will be the bedroom on the main floor. Mine and the children's rooms are upstairs. The Bishop felt this was proper."

Ruby's mind swirled and did not want to work. There was just too much to take in. The book work accounts, the new housekeeper, contemplating closing the store and begin the website to sell her merchandise.

David looked at her expectantly. "You look scared."

"You think so?" She smiled at him then bit her lip as she said, "I am. I-I do not know what to say, David."

"Understandable. How about I give you some time to consider it."

"T-thank you."

"May I ask you a question?"

Ruby nodded in response.

"Where did you get your skills for the computer? It could not have been an easy thing to learn. The Amish schools do not prepare you for such a thing."

Ruby offered him a seat again "I have been taking classes at the library. I began a few years ago to keep track of our reservations." She motioned to the *kaffe* station in the other corner, but David shook his head, so she continued with her story. "Once I learned the software, then came the website building class, then the class where I learned reservations. Before I knew it, the whole farm stay was on there, and we began to really make money."

"You amaze me, Ruby. Will you work for me? Think about it and why don't you let me know next Monday? Right now, I need to get busy. The old *dawdi haus* on my property needs a bit of work. I cannot have my new housekeeper doing such a huge cleaning job. She might not take kindly to us and quit."

David stood, buttoned up his jacket, and walked to the door. He looked back at her and smiled. There was something in the glitter of his blue eyes, which caused her heart to leap in her chest. She felt the change in the room when he walked through the door and closed it softly. She missed him as soon as he was gone.

CHAPTER 11

The last weeks at home truly helped Miriam to feel better. Not one time did she get called away for a birth or an energy healing. The only pregnancy written in her book was her own. In a few months, she would have a little *boppli* in her arms.

Anna's little Abby and Emma were quickly growing. She enjoyed helping her sister-in-law care for the children, but they could be a handful at times.

This afternoon, the *boppli* and their mother were all napping, and Miriam was cooking. Making pie crust filled her with happiness. The aroma of the lard mixed with flour and the actual crumbling it together with her hands gave her deep satisfaction. As a youngster, her crusts were as hard as soapstone, but over the years, and with lots of practice, they became tender and flaky.

So far, she had two chickens roasting and two apple pies cooling. Now, only to finish these crusts and bake them off to use tomorrow for cream pies. The rich fragrance from her cooking filled the room and dropped her back into memories of her *mamm* and *mammi* cooking when she was young. Coming home from school, food smells welcomed her and wrapped the feelings of home around her body. As a grown woman, she experienced these same feelings. Soon, her child would have memories such as hers.

Levi and his brother, Wayne tramped into the back porch. "You two had better take off your boots before coming into the kitchen. I will not have you leaving mud and such all over my freshly mopped kitchen.

"Ok, we hear you," Levi called out to her. Then she heard him muttering something to his brother.

The men hung their winter jackets on hooks, they came into the kitchen in their stocking feet.

"Go warm yourselves by the fire while I'm finishing supper. I will bring you *kaffe* while you wait. Go along."

Levi smiled at her and wrapped his cold arms around her and nuzzled her neck with his cold cheeks. "Levi! Stop," Miriam laughed at his antics. "You are freezing me." Then he kissed her with his cold lips. "You are so bad." Her words were half-jest.

"But I am warmer now," he said and again, kissed her lightly on the lips before going into the front room to join his brother who had found his way to a recliner near the fire.

Miriam shuddered as the thrill of love passed through her. She didn't know what she had done to deserve such love from her husband. They found each other as an older couple, not in their late teens or early twenties like so many of the Amish did. She had felt like she would be an old maid when she reached thirty, then a couple of years later, Levi came into her life. Suddenly, they were creating a family.

She filled the mugs with *kaffe* and took down the remaining chocolate chip cookies she made yesterday placing it all on a tray, she then headed toward the men.

"The new standard-bred horse will be here next week. We will have time to get the information around at the meeting. Then we can see just who we shake out of the bushes as our thieves," Levi said to Wayne, "I would like to get past all this and have those horse thieves locked up."

Miriam stood in the doorway, listening to the conversation. She knew better than to do this. Her father always said if you eavesdropped, you might not like what you hear. In this case, he was undoubtedly right. Miriam did not want Levi involved in trying to catch these criminals. It sounded dangerous to her.

Yes, she knew it was the Amish way to handle problems in their own districts, but sometimes you needed law enforcement as they were trained in this sort of thing. She was glad Asher knew what they were up to, but still hearing their plans made her worry.

Taking a deep breath and sticking on a big smile on her face, Miriam walked into the room with her tray. She set the tray on the table between the chairs where the men were kicked back, enjoying the warmth of the fire.

"I'll tell you when supper is on the table."

"Are Anna and the girls taking a nap?" Wayne asked her as he took the mug full of *kaffe* and blew across the top of it to help cool it.

"They are, so try to be quiet. The *boppli* need rest. It has been a busy day with wash again. Those two go through more diapers!"

"It is a good thing we added more lines in the basement to hold them. Can you imagine how many we will need when our *boppli* comes?" Levi spouted.

Miriam shook her head and said, "At least he will arrive in the summer so we can hang them all out." With that, she went back into the kitchen. Hopefully, Levi did not notice his conversation with Wayne upset her, but it sure did. Why did her husband have to try to solve all the problems in the district? *Please keep Levi safe, dear Lord. We have so much to live for. Thank you for blessing us with this little one I keep close to my heart and bless this boppli with both a mother and father.*

Later that night, Miriam changed into a soft pink flannel nightgown and sat on the edge of the bed, brushing out her long hair while waiting for Levi to finish his shower. He took one every night before going to bed. Levi told her from their first night together that he would never drag hay and horse hair to their bed. Thankfully, he was true to his word.

Levi came into the bedroom. His hair was nearly dry from the brisk towel drying he always gave it. His body smelled of a masculine scent from the soap Miriam bought him at Ruby's store. One of the district ladies, Rachel Schwartz, made it with goat's milk and various essential oils. It smelled so good. Miriam had her own favorite, and soon she would be able to buy her own *kinner* their own made especially for little ones. The woman also made *boppli* clothing which smelled rich in the oils.

"I thought you would be fast asleep." Levi's gentle laughter filled the room. Pulling back the heavy covers topped with a quilt worked-up in shades of blue, he crawled into bed.

Miriam pulled her hair over her shoulder and quickly braided it before slipping into bed beside her husband.

She wanted to talk to him about his involvement in hunting down these horse thieves. How did she even begin? Taking a deep breath, she tried to open up to him, but nothing came out. She tried again with the same results.

Levi rolled over and propped his head on his hand and looked at her. "Is there something you want to say, dear?" he asked softly.

Miriam nodded, and a tear ran down beside her ear. Levi wiped it away and kissed where the trail had been. "You can tell me anything, you know."

Miriam nodded and began again. "I do not want you involved in catching the horse thieves, Levi. It scares me. What if something happened to you?"

Instead of becoming upset, he laughed at her. "Do not worry your pretty little head about this. I have it covered. Between Wayne, the bishop, Ash, and myself, we have a plan. A good one."

Miriam pushed herself into a sitting position and leaned back on the sturdy headboard. "This plan, it still has to do with this new stud horse you have coming in?"

Levi was quiet for a moment, and then he asked her, "Why are you worried?" Miriam's face pulled into a frown.

"It became real to me when I heard you and Wayne talking earlier."

"I am sorry this happened. You do not need the stress, but our plan will work. I know it will, then all this will be over."

CHAPTER 12

The meeting lasted longer than anyone expected. At least the various horse breeders were aware of the problem, one that seemed to be escalating. Levi learned of two more thefts.

The one worrisome note to everyone involved with the horse thefts came down to not knowing where the horses were being kept. Levi suspected, and many of the men agreed, they must be holding them in an Englisch farm, one they did not know.

The only thing the meeting accomplished was to set the plan in motion to catch the thieves. The bishop knew and approved of the trap. Pride filled Levi watching the Bishop tell all of them the new, extremely expensive stud would arrive today at Levi's farm. The bishop wanted to be involved with everything in his district. What a difference a few months made. Old Bishop Yoder was harsh and demanding, while Bishop Eischler loved his community.

Levi snapped the reins of his pacer, wishing they were already at his home. His brother Wayne at least kept the bishop busy in conversation in the back of the buggy. If Bishop Eischler knew Asher waited at the barn, he might not have come with them to set it all in motion, the risk of bringing Asher into their problem went against the Bishop's orders.

Nee, Levi believed the man would detest the police included in the trap. The decision to take this beyond the Amish was Levi's. The danger to his family helped him decide to bring the Englisch law into an Amish problem.

"Levi your brother has some good solid planting ideas for the spring."

"Yes, he does. His help is greatly appreciated."

"You will have more time for training your horses." The bishop smiled as if he was responsible for Wayne coming here. Levi thought about it for a minute and could see the bishop's reasoning. He allowed Wayne to stay. Levi hoped the bishop would approach Wayne about being baptized.

The thought reminded Levi they needed to finish the work on the old farmhouse and get it updated. Levi could feel Miriam's need to have their own home back in order. He was trying, and also wanted them in their home before their *boppli* arrived.

Levi was grateful the road was dry with a minimal amount of ice. So far, the horse had little problems with footing. But he was cautious enough not to push for speed.

The new stud should be arriving in the next hour or so. The bait for the thieves put Levi on edge. The stud, Radar, would make the future breed lines for their farm. He would be relieved when this was over. Worse than the thought of losing the horse was the strain it was putting on Miriam. She really hated the whole plan, and Levi knew it wasn't right for her or the *boppli*.

Levi shook off his worries as he turned the buggy into the yard. He caught sight of Asher as soon as they headed to the barn. His friend since school days opened the barn door for them so Levi could drive the buggy right into the barn.

The bishop huffed beside him, and Levi wished he could disappear. He never faced the bishop's anger and was not looking forward to it.

"We need him, Bishop. These thefts are much more than just one or two in our district, they are increasing at a fast pace. The law must handle them." Levi took a breath and waited for the Bishop to reply. The way he looked at Asher and then Levi was enough to make Levi swallow, hard.

Asher moved up and shook the Bishop's hand, and then began explaining to them all just how dangerous these men had become. Another theft happened last night, resulting in two Amish men being beaten and taken to the hospital.

"Sir, Levi needs our help in apprehending these thieves. Let me show you the equipment we have installed to record them in action. The deputies from Paradise Wells and two other districts will be here, waiting for them."

"What if they don't show." The Bishop was angry, but Levi felt he understood why he had to involve Asher.

"Then we will have to find the thief closer to home. I don't like to think they are so near, but it is a possibility."

The Bishop nodded and seemed to think over the information Asher told them. "You best catch them and soon, Ash. We don't need this danger in our midst."

Before anyone could say more, they heard the truck coming up the drive. "I think your bait just arrived, gentlemen. I will head to the house for a warm drink. I have not seen the new *boppli* Wayne, nor your wife, Levi since hearing the news."

With that said the man left the barn.

Levi and the others snapped out of their surprise over the Bishop and began working on getting the horse into the barn.

Later, after nearly an hour in the house, the bishop returned to the barn. "What a wonderful looking horse." The Bishop never took his attention away from the stud.

Levi smiled, he too couldn't stop watching the animal pawing the ground and prancing around his new stall. The outside wall held a door which opened directly to the large pen that Radar could use. The extra tall walls of the paddock and exercise pen were strong enough to keep him in. Levi had been warned. Radar liked to find his way out of any enclosure. "And the barrier goes down over three feet, so he cannot dig his way out."

"Yes, good work, Levi, I can see where this horse will be a handful. Any thief would want him. I hope everything will work, and this danger will end." The Bishop turned to face Levi. "I am not angry with you, though it was a shock to see Asher here. I should have realized how dangerous this is getting. When will Asher be back for the trap?"

"We decided to wait until the squatters are moved in. They are supposed to all meet at Asher's parent's farm. This way, there will not be any sign of the Englisch on the farm."

The Bishop nodded and then put his hand on Levi's shoulder. "You be careful, Levi. Many people depend on you."

"I will, Bishop."

Together they said a prayer.

Grant us, O Lord, your protection. Within your protection, strength. And within your strength, understanding. And within your understanding, knowledge. And within your knowledge, the power of justice. And within the power of justice, the love of all of Creation. Guide and protect our body, our mind and our best judgment in all things. For you, O Lord, will never leave our side. In this, we trust. Amen.

Levi gave a final wave at the Bishop as his buggy took the turn out of the yard. The Bishop was a good man, and Levi felt hopeful for the district to have such a man.

He pulled the big barn doors closed. Levi needed to make a final sweep of the animals before dinner.

The sound of the smaller door opening caused Levi to spin about. "Miriam. Is something wrong?"

Levi took hold of her hands and gently pulled her to him. "It is good to see you."

He held her to him and moved his hand up and down her back. The tension inside her could be felt by him. Miriam leaned back a small bit and looked up to him. "Do you think this plan will work?"

Levi smiled and rested his chin on the top of her head, inhaling the beautiful scent which belonged only to his wife. "I hope it will. Besides, what thief could pass up such a beautiful horse?"

He laughed softly as she tried to look around him. "Come on, come meet Radar. I have looked for two years to find the perfect stud for our farm."

Miriam moved out of his arms to see the horse. "Oh my, Levi. I have never seen a more beautiful horse."

He stood behind her and held her, "He is that, and I think he will begin our breeding line for us."

Radar came forward, and Miriam pulled a carrot from her pocket. "Yes, you are going to love all the mares waiting for you this spring."

"Oh, wife, you do make a point." His laughter and hers filled the open space of the barn. "It seems he likes girls already. He has not let anyone touch him, and here you stand, holding a carrot as he chomps down the piece you gave him."

"I figured he needed to calm down and what better way than a goodie to eat."

"You will spoil him, Miriam."

"Oh, I intend to."

The look she gave him made Levi want to pick her up and toss her on the nearest haystack.

CHAPTER 13

Anna gave Miriam and Ruby a tour around the house. Including the basement with the double doors leading into the cellar. "There is an opening at the outside directly into the basement. It will help a lot come canning time."

Miriam knew Anna was the one who insisted on getting the squatters into a warm house before she and Wayne moved into the house and made it their new home. Her sister-in-law was entirely right to worry about those people. She thought they all might be relieved when the families got here.

She would check them medically once they got settled, especially the children. Miriam discovered two of the ladies were pregnant. Spring would see a lot of new life on their farm.

Wayne and Levi finished the repairs in the kitchen and heat in the old house. To her surprise, they even updated it with propane.

Ruby told her David and others were already finding jobs for the men. Some of the district ladies wanted to teach the new ladies how to make quilts and other sellable goods to make money in the store. Ruby also wanted to begin going to the craft shows in the area, having these ladies here, would be a big help to Ruby.

She couldn't stop running her hand over the bump of life growing inside of her. Their *boppli* should arrive this summer, and they both could hardly wait for it to join them.

Miriam hid her humor over Anna's authoritative arm wave for herself and Ruby to follow her.

"I want to show the two of you the rooms we set up. I think we can get at least four families, maybe five depending on how many children are involved."

"You have been really busy, Anna."

"You know how it is, Miriam. Our men need some guidance."

Ruby and Miriam looked at each other and mouthed the word guidance. Thankfully neither of them laughed. Miriam decided Anna possessed a great talent to take charge of things. "Whatever the reason, I am glad to see so much progress."

Ruby stepped forward, "Anna, should we begin by getting the curtains up?"

"*Jah*, it will be wonderful. I can go check the twins and put the dishes away which were dropped off. Our neighbors have become quite helpful and are donating many wonderful household items. I think there will be enough for them all."

With the announcement, Anna swirled about and headed downstairs.

"Sister, she is a marvel to have *Gott*en this house in order. It really is beautiful."

"I know Ruby, I have been busy sewing up all the items she needed and taking care of our house. I do not think it would be this ready for anyone if Anna hadn't taken charge. Levi said there was more to her than anyone knew to suspect."

"Well, he is right."

Anna called up the back stairs to the kitchen for them to come down for a moment.

"Here Ruby, let's put the curtains in here for now."

Once downstairs, they followed Anna's call from the basement.

"Oh good, you are up there. Come down here. I wanted to show you both how large the basement is.

When the sisters walked into the basement, Anna said, "We will need to string some clotheslines for the rest of the winter. Do you think we can find a washer? I discovered some faucets over in the corner we could use to hook up to a washer."

Ruby spoke up, "I will put a notice up on the board at the shop, it should get the word out."

"Oh thank you, it has been working quite well since you made the notice board."

"Anna? When will the families be arriving?"

"Levi and Wayne made contact with the families when we were leaving, and the Bishop with Wayne have been back. Levi said the men from your district, or should I say ours, now, should be ready to pick up and bring them here in two days."

Miriam came back from checking out the rest of the basement. "I am so worried about this whole thing. I will be relieved to have it done and out of our lives."

She tried not to get upset, but it became too difficult to ignore. Levi was in danger, and it needed to stop. If they did not catch them, Miriam knew she would not be quiet about it. She refused to stay with Anna and Wayne that night.

"Miriam, what did you find over there?"

She smiled at Ruby, understanding she was trying to take her attention away from the worry. "We need to get shelves up for the canning. There is a lot of room, and even after they leave, it will be wonderful to have the storage."

"Oh yes, Miriam. You are so right about it, I will make sure to note it for Wayne. Once planting is over, he will be able to make some."

Anna's smile became contagious.

"Oh, look over there, Anna. There is an outside door. I have always felt they lent safety to the inhabitants. I will make sure the doors are cleared of any debris."

The girl giggled, and Miriam looked at her in question.

"Miriam, we do think alike. I cleared the door the other day to be sure anyone can get in or out."

"If everyone could take a seat in the other room we will begin with the meeting." Levi's voice carried over all the heads of people in the kitchen. Miriam smiled and hoped they would listen, she needed to sit down.

After cooking breakfast for the crowd, she was exhausted. She wondered how all these ladies fared so well during their pregnancies. She still felt tired all the time. Even eating small snacks almost every hour hadn't boosted her energy.

She looked down and rubbed her *boppli's* large ball, Miriam almost laughed, she couldn't see her feet. She was bigger than most at this stage. She sighed and refused to worry over it all.

People were not leaving the kitchen. Deciding men never like to listen to anyone, she picked up her pad of paper and walked through many conversations saying, "the pads of paper and pens are there on the counter if you need them."

She smiled to herself when the men walked behind her, slow that they were, but at least they were finally moving, and she could sit and watch them filter in. Miriam rubbed her lower back to help ease the pain. Thoughts of Levi massaging her back tonight brought a silent smile to her face.

She felt his presence behind her just before his hands gently squeezed her shoulders. His warm breath brushed her ear as he whispered, "You look like an angel with not so nice thoughts in your pretty head."

Miriam's cheeks flared in heat, and it was all she could do not to laugh out loud. He gave her shoulders one last squeeze before moving away. Since she began staying home, their relationship flourished and felt so beautiful. At first, she worried she made the wrong decision but becoming close to Levi meant the world to her, she would not change a thing.

Ruby and Anna came to sit with Miriam in the front row of the ladies' seats. They all settled down when Levi walked up to the front with the Bishop.

"This meeting is to keep everyone informed of the progress we are making. The house for the families is basically finished. We are waiting for the new heater to be hooked up today, the other one failed to keep working. But, all the major repairs are completed thanks to the extra help these last couple days. Thank you."

Levi smiled and let the Bishop take over the meeting.

The Bishop raised his hands to gain attention again. "Everyone, I have some fantastic news, I have been able to speak to all six family heads to learn of each of the circumstances of their shunning and how they feel about coming back to the district and our church.

I will tell you, each of these family's conditions is due to the last bishop. Also, I've researched all the records, and it seems as though all the men were shunned before being baptized. They all want to come back. There is one family that is ready to make this step and will do so at our spring service, Wayne and Anna Miller, please come forward."

The whole room was silent, and Miriam couldn't stop smiling. "This is so wonderful, Ruby. They are taking the baptism classes."

Her sister reached over and took hold of her hand. "It really is, Miriam."

The Bishop continued and said a prayer for the couple and their future in the district.

"You all know Wayne, and Anna Miller insisted on bringing the families into their home. We will be investigating the other families and their former homes to see what can be done. Wayne will be farming his family's land."

With a final prayer, the Bishop moved on to other business. "Most of the men will be working on David Fisher's land this spring. It isn't far off, and we hope these people can heal. One family will stay in my *dawdi haus*. This is a man and his sister. We have two bedrooms there so this will accommodate them quite well. Another family will stay with Luke and Irene Temple. They are both quite aged and need help. The man will take care of the animals and small farm while his wife will maintain the house and meals. The Temple's are so happy to have the younger couple stay with them. It is the best of both worlds. The elderly readily accept the help because they feel they are helping in their own way as well."

The meeting continued with different attendees addressing their part of the project. Wayne had a list of items they needed for the spring. He read the list of various tools and equipment.

The women remained quiet while the men discussed the problems and successes at this point. It was decided the families were moving in later today and everyone who came was ready to go get them and their belongings. Most came with wagons so everything could be hauled at one time.

When the men left, the women held their own less formal meeting. Anna led the meeting.

"...that should do it. I want to thank you all so much. It is wonderful to be here."

Surprisingly, all the women stood up and clapped for Anna. It was heart swelling to feel all the love in the room.

Everyone quickly gathered up the last items to take to the house. Miriam told them to load the wagon up. Ruby and Anna would drive the wagon over, and Miriam would follow with the buggy.

The air was more than brisk, and Miriam was relieved the families would be inside tonight. It was supposed to be below freezing in the single digits. Miriam prayed they had the new heater up and running. Levi told her if it were not hooked up, the old wood stove and heaters would be lit for heat. One thing about their men, they knew how to get things done

"Especially my love." Miriam would not be surprised if the wood stoves were already lit to bring up the heat in the old place. "It really is a beautiful home."

"What is it, sister?"

"Anna's home, I think it is beautiful, and the families will love it."

"You are right. Now move over I am driving."

"What about the wagon?"

"Anna already recruited another lady to help her. She certainly gets things done."

They both laughed softly over the truth.

"Do you know Ruby, Anna is the one who insisted the wood stove and heaters remain in each room and to stay and be functional.

CHAPTER 14

"I think we have finished the last room." Miriam could tell Anna wasn't overjoyed. "What is wrong, Anna?"

"The whole place looks marvelous, except it isn't clean."

"Ahh, yes, well this can happen once the families are moved in."

"I know, it would have been nice..." Anna spun about in front of Miriam and Ruby. "Did you hear the sounds outside? It is too early for anyone to be arriving."

Miriam did not wait for Anna to snap out of her musing, it was way too cold a day to leave people waiting outside. "Hello, Carly?"

"Yes, oh my Miriam you are getting so big!" Miriam finally got over being stunned when Carly hugged her. "I am late, but we made it. Come on in ladies."

A parade of women with step stools, brooms, mops, and buckets filled with cleaners and more, came into the kitchen. Anna stood silent on one side of the table, with Ruby who couldn't stop laughing and Miriam.

Carly went right over to Ruby, "Where should we begin?"

"I think it best to get the rooms upstairs done first in case some of the families get here early."

"Could you show the ladies, I need to meet Anna before she faints."

Ruby giggled again and led the ten to twelve ladies up the main stairs to put them to work. She patted Miriam on the back as she passed.

Miriam moved forward once the kitchen cleared. She took hold of her friend's hand, and they walked over to the still silent Anna. "Anna, please meet Carly, our Englisch friend, she lives at the farm stay."

"Oh my! I have heard so much about you, Carly." Anna's shyness didn't last long. When the girl lifted her hand for Carly shake it, Carly pulled her into a big hug.

"We are family, Anna, hugs are mandatory."

"Anna, I think Carly has a surprise for you."

"I certainly do, you see, Ruby told me about the last crew today to get the place finished, and I picked cleaning. I have my friends here, and they all want to help, so here we are. I grabbed the women after your meeting. They call this a *frolic*. They tell me this is fun to do. We work fast and have a system, so we should be done quickly, I hope it will be soon enough."

"Oh, yes, it will be fine."

"Good, I will keep you informed." Carly headed for the stairs.

Miriam called after her, "We will get a pot of *kaffe* going."

Carly called back, "I have a few dozen muffins in the car."

"Oh, wonderful, I do love your muffin's."

Anna raced out the door to get the goodies as Miriam began making a large pot of *kaffe*. "Carly still surprises me."

Miriam looked up at the ceiling and smiled, "the house is full once again."

True to her word, Carly and her crew were done in just over an hour. The place smelled like lemons and berries and looked shiny and new. Anna walked from one room to the next unable to stop smiling. The ladies finished up the dishes from their *kaffe* and muffins and left with a promise to Anna to come back for the quilting class.

Carly pushed up from her chair and smiled at everyone. "Anna, is there anything you need help with before I go?"

"My goodness, no, thank you so much, Carly, for all you and your friends got done. The place looks beautiful, they are going to love it."

"I am sure they will. If you do find you need help with anything, just let me know."

"I will Carly."

"Oh! I almost forgot. I have some wonderful and exciting news." She looked from Anna to Miriam and Ruby. "I have purchased Mr. Hamlin's bakery." Carly stayed silent a moment to let her words sink in. "If you need me, this is where I will be starting at three in the morning as he is training me how to make all the bread, cookies and cakes, and other goodies. My main bakery item is going to be the muffins, they are what my bakery will specialize in. I have a feeling they are going to be extremely popular in town and out. My first customer is Hannah."

They all shook their heads in agreement over the truth.

All of the congratulations didn't last too long as they all heard the wagons coming up the hill from the main road.

"I best scoot out of here before they all scramble for a spot."

"Carly, take the back way to my home, the road is clear."

"Good idea, Miriam. Alright, I'm out and away."

They all waved her goodbye and waited for the first wagon to come up the hill.

"I think this is the last of it all." Anna sank into the kitchen chair.

Miriam wanted to laugh but was too exhausted to do so. "Best rest a bit, Anna. Ruby is still upstairs."

"Without you two, I never would have made it today, so thank you."

"I am just relieved they are out of this storm, it is so cold out there. Levi called and said I should stay put, he will be here to pick Ruby and me up."

"I know, Wayne made it home, just barely. He was practically frozen. He said he had to get home to get all the animals inside and bedded down for the night. He also told me Levi decided to stay out in the barn to keep the heaters going for the animals."

"He is like that. I can hardly wait to see how he is with our *boppli*. Levi is so excited for the child to come."

"It must run in the family." Anna laughed softly and drew a tired smile from Miriam.

She really wanted to get home and sleep in Levi's arms, he would keep her warm, the weather decreed otherwise. The latest report said it was ten below with the wind chill down to minus thirty.

"You should go and lie down and get some sleep. I promise to wake you as soon as Levi arrives."

Miriam couldn't prevent her laughter over Anna's weighty announcement. "Did we get a final count on the children? I did, we have two *boppli*, four toddlers, and one nine-year-old, along with eight adults and two ladies are carrying *boppli*. This is what I call a full house."

"I never got a chance to count them all, probably best I didn't, I may have fainted over the enormity of it all. We may need to increase the house gardens again."

"True, Anna, we just might."

"Not right now, we aren't." Ruby moved behind Miriam and massaged her sister's shoulders and neck. "They are all finally asleep."

"Thank goodness, Ruby." Anna pushed herself up, "I am going to go and collapse while I can. G'night, you two and thank you again."

They both wished her a good night as well.

Ruby kept working on her sister's shoulders. "You are so tight, Miriam."

"I think it was all those trips up the stairs and back. I finally had to call a halt to my traveling up there."

"I am glad you did."

Miriam covered her sister's hand on her shoulder. "I hear the carriage."

"Yes, that is Levi. I heard about the storm from Wayne. I am glad he made it home in time to take care of the livestock. We were right to send everyone home as soon as the wagon was unloaded. Otherwise, we would be sleeping on clean floors."

Miriam stood up with Ruby's help and giggled softly, "Carly is a wonder."

"And such a wonderful friend to have, sister."

"Yes, she is."

Together they headed to the mudroom under the stairwell to get their cloaks and hats on to get home.

CHAPTER 15

Levi stopped pacing and went to the window to check the barn once again. "Nothing." The failure hissed through his lips. The sun would come up in half an hour or so, but the thieves never showed.

He knew Asher would stay hidden in case they were watching. Levi was anxious to wake Miriam and tell her what happened. More than likely they would do this again tonight. If thieves failed to show again, Levi was not sure what to do next.

Miriam was angry with him and refused to go over to Wayne and Anna's place, another night would not help the situation.

He would ask her to stay upstairs tonight, at least she would not be downstairs. He didn't want her to be so upset because it was not right in her condition.

Levi smiled, remembering how big she had become this last month. He wondered about the possibility of twins. Excitement filled him at the thought, but it could also be as simple as a missed count on how far along she was. They both agreed she could plausibly have the *boppli* in a few months.

It made Levi think about planting. The ground was nearly thawed. A couple of warm evenings like the last few and they could be planting by next week. He needed to get his acres planted for the grains and hays he required for next winter. All the men in their district took days to help each other plow and at times, plant. Their individual success came about from the help of many. Then the vast vegetable garden for the home, he and Miriam both decided to plant twice as much than last year so all the new people will have enough food as well. Both Anna and Miriam gave Wayne and himself a list for planting.

Once it was done, he would help Wayne finish up the farm planting.

Levi laughed to himself. Anna and Miriam were quite a team. They already figured out what and how much canning they could do this year, and they had a lot of help to get it all done.

One request made both Wayne and him stutter a bit...Lambs. Neither he nor his brother ever remembered having any sheep, though Miriam did say they should really investigate alpacas. As Miriam told him the fleece is much better, and it could become a cash crop for the farms. She already researched them, as she knew exactly how many acres they needed for the alpacas or the sheep. To be honest, Levi liked the idea of the alpaca.

He stopped pacing when he heard the backdoor open and shut.

"Levi? It is Asher."

"I am here."

Asher turned to face him, and Levi could see his friend was frustrated.

"Ash, I will be okay if you want to try it for a couple more nights."

"I think we should."

"Yes, maybe they have moved on, but we won't know unless we keep trying."

"You're right, Levi. How is Miriam going to handle the news, though?"

Levi gave a huff, "I am already bracing myself."

"It should be safe enough, Levi."

"Yes, better than letting her get all worked up."

"When is she due?"

"We figure June, but only the *boppli* will know for sure."

"The men are gone. Do you need some help with the animals? I will stay, I don't want to leave the place unguarded."

"*Jah*, it would be good."

Together they left the house to go to the barn.

Levi took the time to feed his new stud. Radar needed to become used to him for all his care. Of course, Miriam and Radar were bonding. The big guy practically walked on eggs around her. Levi concluded the horse knew she was carrying a child,

CHAPTER 16

"The air is heavy with the smell of newly turned earth, all refreshed and ready to cradle the seeds dropped in its care."

Miriam moved her hands around as if she could catch the air. Levi never saw her look so beautiful and loved. "You best sit down and eat this wonderful lunch you brought me."

"Hmm, I guess you are right." She looked back at him and smiled. "Our *boppli* loves it out here, Levi. Oh my, he is rolling over."

Levi reached up to feel the baby change direction. "Yes, he is getting ready and wants to be out here with us."

Miriam came to sit beside him, picking up the plate he filled for her. "You better eat as well, Levi. Your day is not over."

"True, but David's help these past two days made a huge difference. I wonder if Wayne would have made it without his help."

"He is a true friend."

"Yes, he is. I will be over at his place plowing the fields for the next few days. All of us should be ready to plant after this week. David and his crew are at Matthew and Hannah's today, so we all meet at David's in the morning."

"I am sure you will all be plowing and getting his land ready for planting."

"Are you and Anna ready to seed the house gardens?"

"Oh yes, we are going to get Anna's first as it is bigger. She has the whole garden plotted out in a diagram, so we know what goes where. She also diagramed our garden as well. If the land agrees, we will have a fine harvest to can for everyone, even David increased his house garden. I believe Matthew did the same."

"Yes he did, almost doubled it. Ruby and Hannah are looking toward bringing in can goods to sell in the store this fall."

"Oh Levi, that will be wonderful. The various ladies have their family recipes, and I am sure they will be excited to put them on display."

Levi laid down on his back on the blanket, he pulled Miriam over him carefully. "If you think the *boppli* is impatient, I am worse." His laughter brought a smile to his wife's lips. "You are so lovely, Miriam, I hope we have a little girl who looks just like her mother."

"Hmm, maybe, this *boppli* feels strong like a boy."

"He will be fine as well, but we will need to try for a girl."

Her laughter fanned his face as she came closer and placed a light kiss on the tip of his nose.

"We both need patience, Levi."

"*Jah*, we certainly will. I am sure girl or boy, they will keep us up at all times. Miriam, I promise to help change diapers and with the feedings."

"Good I will need the help."

Levi hated to leave her, but he needed to finish his field so he could move on to David's land. The man said they formed a coalition farming like this. He would not be against it for future plantings.

"I need to get back to the plowing to stay on schedule." He looked around as he helped her stand up. "Miriam, where is your buggy? I don't see it."

"I walked up, this is too beautiful a day to ride." Miriam placed her hand on his cheek. "I will be fine, Levi, honest. It is good for me to walk at this time."

Levi felt conflicted, "Yes, I know, but I worry about you."

"I will head for the house on this path. Do you have your phone?"

Levi touched his top pocket. "I do,"

"I will call you when I get to the house. I should be there within the hour. Okay?"

"*Jah*, go and be sure to call." Levi reached around her and took the basket and blanket from her hold. "I will bring this home with me."

He could see she wanted to argue, but then she snapped her lips close. "Fine, I will call. Love you."

He watched her for a couple minutes before turning to gather his horses for the plowing. "Take care, my love."

Miriam took her time getting home, the day just felt perfect, especially after winter. As she approached the yard, she pulled out her phone. "Hi, I am at home."

"Good I was beginning to worry."

"One doesn't walk fast with this load." Her laughter filled the air. "Oh, I almost forgot to ask you. Radar is having a fit, he wants out, may I put him in the pasture?"

"I don't know Miriam, he can be ornery."

"I know, but he stays calm near me. I have decided that a small girl raised him. I must remind him of her."

"You are probably right. Just make sure the gate is locked or we will have the horse's colts all over the district."

"I will be careful. I may sit out there and watch Radar run."

"Good, I will be home soon."

"I will be out here or in the house."

"Love you."

Miriam ended the call with a smile and headed up to the barn.

When Radar saw her, he let out a heartful whinny. "Yes, you had a wonderful girl care for you. I am glad I can make the loss better my big man." She rubbed the blaze which went from his forehead to his nose. "My husband really knows horses."

Miriam unhooked his lead from stall door and attached it to his halter. "You want to go for a run?"

His nodded yes, Miriam eventually closed her mouth and opened his stall door. "Be good Radar. We could make this a daily outing for you." When they reached the pasture, his head was moving in all directions, discovering his surroundings. He walked in with her, never once pulling her. She closed the gate and then unlatched him. "You can run now, Radar. Go on it is okay, have fun."

Miriam watched as he backed away from her then took off, "He is so beautiful, my goodness look at his tail standing straight up."

She never thought of moving out of the pasture, sure he would not hurt her. "Oh, he is pacing. Wait until I tell Levi."

He stood still when he came to the end of the pasture. He started calling then stopped as if waiting for someone to answer, and they did. Miriam looked to her left where she knew the mares were pastured. She could not see them, but she did hear their answering his call. She quickly looked at Radar, he called again and then reared up pawing the air. *He indeed held a magnificence about him.*

He took off pacing about the open field. Miriam felt confident she could leave him now, and he would be fine. She rechecked the gate lock one more time before leaving him. He did seem to settle down a bit and began eating some fresh grass. "I will be back in about an hour."

He called back to her as if he understood, causing Miriam's laughter to float on the breeze. "A truly wonderful day."

CHAPTER 17

Levi and Asher faced each other as they drank coffee and ate pie at the Paradise Wells coffee shop. "I'm glad you could meet me this morning, Levi," Asher said, then he took a bite of the peach pie and followed it up with steaming coffee.

Levi leaned over toward his friend and asked, "Have there been more horses missing?"

Shaking his head, Ash offered, "No. Nothing. It's been over a month since we tried to surprise them in your barn. Not one report of anything on this side of the state. Everything has stopped."

"It makes a person wonder why," Levi said.

"True. I've been wondering if the thieves are in our midst. Like some of the newcomers back into the Amish fold." Asher's brows knit in concern.

"*Ach,* surely not. I have met all the families, and no one seems to be the sort to do this."

The bells attached to the cafe door rang as Bishop Eischler stepped in. He looked around and spotted, Levi and Asher. He walked toward them.

"Take a seat, Bishop," Levi said. He pulled out a chair beside him, then motioned to the waitress to bring another cup of *kaffe.*

The bishop spoke up, raising his voice, he told the girl to bring him an apple pie.

"You two looked in serious conversation when I walked in. Has there been more missing horses?"

Asher shook his head and put down the coffee mug. "Nothing. It has me worried. Why did all this stop? I told Levi I wondered if some of the new people you have in your fold might have been involved, and now their lives are calming down and they have work, the thieving may have stopped because of this."

The Bishop shook his head. "I do not think this could be the case."

"I just do not understand. Could it be the thieves were on to us? Someone saw the men hiding the night we tried to apprehend them?"

Asher scraped up the crust crumbs on his plate. The waitress arrived with the bishop's pie and coffee. Asher cleared his throat as she turned to leave. "How about bringing me a piece of apple pie, it looks fantastic."

"Sorry, Asher, that was the last piece. We have another of your favorites, strawberry rhubarb. We are trying the pies from the new girl who bought the bakery. I swear, we run out of them fast. What goes even faster are her muffins. You have to be here early if you want one."

"Ok, bring me her pie. It's a long time until lunch, and I'm still hungry."

Levi poured more cream into his refilled coffee. "If you ask me, I think everything is going great. All the men have jobs, and the women are working hard to help Anna with the big house and cooking for all the people there. Four families living together can be quite difficult if someone shirks their duties,"

The Bishop laughed under his breath. "Have you met John and Susan Lantz?"

The younger men shook their heads.

"John is the laziest man I've ever encountered. Once he is back from working at David Fisher's farm, he comes back to the *dawdi haus,* leaves his horse tied up under the tree then goes to bed leaving his sister to take care of the horse." Bishop Eischler shook his head. "The sister, Ruth, seems to be nice, but overworked. I am not offering gossip here, men, I just want you to be aware of this and also, Levi, maybe Miriam could drop in on Ruth. She is much too thin, and her face is lined with worry. Maybe she is ill."

"Or worn out from doing all the work for that worthless brother of hers," Asher laughed. Suddenly, his phone buzzed in his pocket. He fiddled with a clasp on the case, then spoke into the phone. He stood and then walked to the back of the cafe, where there were empty tables for privacy. After a few moments, he returned to their table and sat to finish his pie and coffee. "I'll have to leave in a bit. There has been a car crash ten miles south of here. Scotty, my new deputy, has it handled, but I want to offer him support."

Asher left the cafe, and Levi and the bishop continued talking. Suddenly, the bishop looked up and clapped his hands together. "I forgot to tell you. I had a single fellow come by looking for work. Jim Hooley, he said his name was. He looked as tattered as the rest of the folks, so I am letting him stay in my barn. I can use a hand with my land as spring is here. I certainly hope all these people work out and come to baptism."

Levi nodded. "I sure hope so as well."

The men sat quietly and finished their mid-morning snacks.

CHAPTER 18

Miriam could not sleep. She tossed this way and that way, and no matter how she turned, the baby moved and would not settle. Sighing, she sat up. Not wanting to awaken Levi, she slid from the mattress and put on her slippers with leather soles. The thick heavy wrap hung from the back of the door. Miriam trudged to the opening, slipped on her robe then quietly pushed at the door. The words, *please stay asleep, Levi,* cried through her mind. She left it open, not wanting to chance him hearing the latch.

The house was shrouded in darkness but every few moments, distant lightning flashed as an early spring storm began to roll in. Miriam's vision in the dark was good, so she filled the tea kettle with a mug full of water and turned on the propane stove. It would not take long to have a cup of chamomile tea. Hopefully, it will help her to relax and get to sleep.

Sitting at the table, she rubbed her ample belly. Miriam worked with expectant mothers, but she did not recognize until her own body stretched into something she did not know, just how painful the changes were. And sharing your body with another being was nearly frightening. Smiling, she patted her baby and whispered, "Little one only a few more weeks, and we will see each other."

The water rumbled in the pot. Miriam rinsed out her teacup, which was sitting in the sink. She had not washed up the few dishes which remained after their supper snacking. The tin which held the tea bags sat on the counter, and after taking one out, she walked back to the table. After a few minutes dunking the bag up and down, she took a sip. The smooth, precious liquid accompanied by the sweet smell of flowers relaxed her immediately.

As Miriam sat waiting for the sensation of sleep to overwhelm her, she watched the lightning come closer and closer. Suddenly, Radar began to fuss in his stall. He did not sound happy at all. Her love for the horse caused her to stand. Looking at the clock, she saw it was three a.m.

Grabbing an apple from the fridge, she took off toward the barn.

A few drops of cold rain hit her head as she ran toward the sliding barn door. As she approached it, a flash of lightning illuminated the area. The barn door was open.

She stopped. Had Levi forgotten to close it? The notion did not feel right. He would never do this. Of course, she remembered hollering out to him earlier when supper was ready. So, maybe he forgot.

Walking into the dark barn, she heard the horse kicking at the stall and making sounds that curdled her blood. What was the matter with that darn horse?

"Radar! What is your problem?" Miriam spoke to him in a calming voice. "I brought you an apple. It is only a storm."

As she neared the stall, she saw a tall man leading Radar into the central part of the barn. "What's the problem in there, Jim?"

Miriam turned and caught sight of two more men as more lightning seared through the sky. They had a horse trailer backed up to the smaller back door of the barn. They must have come up from the gravel road at the side of the barn.

The horse thieves.

Miriam reached into her robe pocket. Her cell phone rested there. Grabbing it, she held it up. "Get out of here right now, or I am calling the police!"

"No Miriam, get down!" Levi rushed up behind her, pulling her behind him.

Suddenly, a flash split the darkness, and the sound of a gun going off made her drop to the floor. Was she shot? Moving her body around, she did not feel any pain. Looking up, she saw the men race from the barn with Radar right behind them as the terrified horse made his escape.

A boom of thunder and the flash of lightning shook the ground. And on the ground lay Levi. Blood seeping from his chest.

"No!" Miriam screamed into the night.

Terror filled her, but she had sense enough to dial 911. After gasping the information into the phone, she dropped and crawled to Levi.

She could detect a faint erratic pulse in his neck, and his breath was shallow and rapid. None of her medical knowledge came to her mind. Nothing but her healing methods.

Pulling at each side of Levi's shirt, Miriam saw a dark round wound near the middle of his chest where blood was pouring out. She remembered she needed to keep him warm. Tearing off her robe, she put it over her husband, then looking to the heavens she began to pray. *Oh, please, dear heavenly father. Please let me keep Levi. The boppli and I need him so much. Place your hands over mine and guide me to heal his dreadful wound. Please, God. Please.*

As she prayed, the sound of sirens grew closer and closer. Help was coming. Miriam continued praying and holding her hands on Levi's gunshot wound.

The barn door slid all the way open, and an ambulance raced inside, its lights flooded the area. Three men ran toward her, two of them with a gurney. They were followed by Asher.

Miriam watched as if she were above the room. The voices were faint. "Mrs. Miller move back so we can help your husband."

She shook her head. No way she could stop the healing. She would know when it was time. Another man touched Levi's neck. He looked to his partner and shook his head. "There is nothing we can do for him.:

"No!" Miriam screamed. "We have to get to the hospital."

Asher squatted at her side. "Come on, Miriam, let him go."

She violently shook her head. "No! No way." She had to keep on. This was the only way for him to survive.

Asher looked at the EMTs. "Load them both up into the ambulance and get them to the hospital. She will feel we tried to help him."

The men loaded Levi onto the gurney with Miriam never raising her hands. The EMTs lifted her as well and Levi.

Sirens screamed, but Miriam could barely hear them. She prayed for Levi continually. Then God spoke to her. *So do not fear, for I am with you; do not be dismayed, for I am your God. I will strengthen you and help you; I will uphold you with my righteous right hand.*

Miriam felt a jostle, and one of the EMTs spoke to her telling her they were in the emergency room. Never leaving Levi, she kept her hands in place. She saw the sadness in Asher's eye as he took in the scene, the EMTs looked worse. They thought her actions futile.

Doctors and medical people moved around Levi. Meriam deepened her trance-like state, and in her mind, she saw Levi tossing a blond-haired little girl in the air. He smiled down at her. At that moment, she knew Levi would survive.

"We've got a faint pulse." A doctor spoke excitedly. "Let's get him to OR, STAT!"

A nurse moved Miriam aside and softly told her of the excellent care they would give Levi, and for her to go to the waiting area. Miriam had no idea where it was at. All she knew was her beloved husband was moving down the hallway to an elevator.

She closed her eyes and blinked tears. When she opened them, her sister, Ruby, stood looking at her. "How is he?" she asked softly. Her face was white.

"They are taking him to surgery."

"But Asher told me the EMTs said he was gone."

"No. Mammi, God and I healed him enough to get him back."

The last thing Miriam heard was Ruby scream as Miriam's water broke and she fainted, dropping to the floor in front of Ruby.

CHAPTER 19

Miriam began to awake. Pain screamed through her body. She opened her eyes and found herself inside a curtained area.

"Miriam. You are awake!"

Only a moan slipped past her lips. Why was Ruby standing by her bed? Suddenly, pain ripped through her heart. It hurt worse than her belly. "Levi, where is he, sister." The look on Ruby's face made her heart feel like it was skipping beats. A machine at the head of her bed let out a blaring sound in time with her heart. "Someone shot him in the barn. I need to go to him. Help me up." She struggled to sit up, but the pain ripped through her again.

Ruby gently laid her back on the bed. "The doctors have Levi in surgery. A nurse spoke to me thirty minutes ago. He was holding his own. The gunshot nicked his heart, and the doctors are working on getting the bleeding stopped. Your healing hand kept him from dying, Miriam. Now we let the medical people make him well."

Miriam shook her head. "He has to make it, he has to for our daughter."

"You just concentrate on bringing this *boppli* into the world. Your water broke, and you passed out from the stress of all this."

"*Nee! It is too soon!*"

"Your doctor thinks the *boppli* will be fine, but there is a problem."

Miriam groaned then asked, "What is it, sister? What is wrong with our *boppli*?"

Ruby laughed under her breath. "There are two babies. Both of them are large. To keep all three of you safe, they want to do a cesarean.

Dilation has begun, so they want to take you in shortly. They were waiting for you to wake up to sign the papers."

Tears poured down Miriam's cheeks. How had everything turned out so wrong? Not only did she worry about Levi, now she has two children to bring up. Two. It explained so much. Her size, the painful movements of the babies."

A tall, thin woman with short-cropped hair walked into the cubical between the curtains. "The nurses tell me you're awake. I'm your doctor, Dr. Carlisle. I'm here to tell you what's happening with your babies. Did you know you were having twins?"

Miriam shook her head. "*Nee,* we home birth in our district unless something is wrong. I am the midwife of our district."

The woman smiled at her and offered her hand to shake. "From one professional to another, something *is* wrong. You are built too small to deliver these babies the natural way. A cesarean is the only way, and we need to do this immediately. You have a belt around you, which keeps track of the babies heart rates. The largest baby is fine, but the smaller one is struggling each time you have a contraction."

Ruby presented Miriam with a clipboard where the permission paperwork lay, awaiting her signature. Miriam took the pen and asked Ruby, "Will you show me where to sign?"

In moments the papers were in the doctor's hands, and nurses replaced her. Swarming the bed, they readied Miriam for transport. "Ruby, come with me. I cannot do this alone. With Levi in surgery, I need strength from you."

Ruby looked at the nurses who nodded their permission.

The elevator carried them up three floors to the operating suites. Miriam grasped a nurses' hand and asked, "Is my husband near here?"

The older woman nodded. "Yes, he is in the room next to yours. Of course, your recovery room will be in obstetrics, and your husband will be in intensive care. All of us will take good care of your family."

The nurse gave her comfort as she was wheeled into the delivery room.

Miriam was no more than settled under a bright light when the doctor walked in. She spoke to another doctor who had the nurses turn Miriam to the side. After a sharp poke in the back, she returned to a prone position.

Ruby was dressed in a gown and stood by Miriam's bedside holding her hand. Miriam felt nothing, and in moments, she heard a baby cry. "This one is a boy. She could see the doctor hand him over to one of the nurses. "She'll bring him right back to you. Now let's see who we have waiting."

In just a bit another howl came from the second baby. "This one is a girl. She's the smaller of the two." Another nurse took her across the room to join her twin, but just as she arrived, the other nurse brought back her brother to Miriam. He was cleaned off and wrapped in a soft blue blanket He had a sweet little hat on his head. Miriam smiled and reached for him. "Come little one. Let me see you." He was beautiful with smooth skin and full lips which pulled into a wail. Miriam laughed. She was accustomed to the newly arrived *boppli*. Finding him crying was the best news.

Suddenly, she worried about her daughter. Miriam did not hear her crying. She wondered if the nurses were taking longer with her than they had with her brother. Just as her pulse began to speed in her veins, the nurse came with the *boppli*. This one covered in pink. Settling into Miriam's other arm, her daughter let out a howl louder and longer than her brother.

"Oh, we are all going to have so much fun together. Just wait until you meet your *Daed,* he will love you both so much."

Ruby stood by. Her eyes were filled with so much love for her sister and her *boppli*. Miriam turned her attention to her sister. "Ruby, please go see if you can find out what is happening with Levi? I am so scared!"

The doctor stepped up to them and said, "No need for her to do this. They just called from the recovery room. He's out of surgery. Soon, he will be taken to intensive care."

"Will I be able to go to him then?"

"Absolutely not, Miriam. You just had surgery yourself. I'll see how you are tomorrow. If you are recovering well, someone will take you to him in a wheelchair. For now, rest and enjoy your babies. They are both fine. I expected them to be preemies, but they show no indication of being early. These are full-term babies."

Relief flooded Miriam. "Thank you, doctor Carlisle. Can my sister stay in my room with me and the *boppli* tonight?"

Laughing, the doctor replies, "No. The babies are going to the nursery. Now, if your sister wants to stay with you, she may do so, but not the babies."

Miriam nodded in compliance. She began to nod off. The nurses came for her *boppli*, and someone else began pushing the bed out of the operating room. Ruby walked behind on the way to Miriam's room.

CHAPTER 20

Ruby sat bolt upright in the recliner beside Miriam's bed. She began to doze off when Miriam screamed. Jumping to her feet, she stood beside her sister whose eyes were starting to open.

"A bad dream?" Ruby asked.

"*Nee!* It was the bad man shooting both me and Levi."

"Asher will find them. He has a call out for all police departments to watch for the pickup and horse trailer." Miriam pushed herself up in the bed. Looking at the clock, she saw it was nearly six p.m. "I do not remember any details, sister."

"Which is to be expected. You have gone through a lot. I checked on Levi a while ago. They have given him medicine which puts him into a coma."

"A coma?"

"Until his heart is stronger. Just think of it as he is asleep."

Miriam nodded. "Are the *boppli* okay?"

Ruby saw the love pour from Miriam's gaze. She loved her little ones so much. "Strong, the nurse said when I asked her. I could hear them crying outside the nursery. That pair is going to keep you on your toes."

Two meals arrived for them brought to them from the hospital kitchen. Removing the plastic lids, they found a slice of limp beef roast smothered with a thin, clear gravy. The broccoli looked overcooked and gray. Store bought bread sat in a bag, and a little box of milk finished off the meal.

"I am not sure I can eat this," Miriam said in a whisper.

Ruby shook her head. "Me too. It looks disgusting. Since we are in the big city of Lancaster, would you like something from a fast food store? I'll fetch it for us."

"How? You do not have a car."

Ruby patted her sister's hand. "There are posters for something called Uber. I think it is like we have in our district. You call, and a person comes to pick you up. What do you want to eat?"

Miriam chuckled then her brows pulled together in a guilty look. "A Big Mac, fries, and a strawberry shake?"

"*Wonderbarr!* I will have the same." Ruby bent over the bed and kissed her sister's forehead. "Just sleep while I'm gone. Dream of the smell of greasy food."

Ruby took the elevator to the third-floor obstetrics area. When the doors opened, the waiting room was filled with people from the district. They were concerned for Miriam and Levi.

Asher approached and took her by the elbow and led her to a small room off the lobby where doctors met with families.

"Have a seat, Ruby," he said. Noticing the bags she carried, he went on, "I won't keep you long. I can see you have food for both you and Miriam.

She nodded but did not offer any declarations.

"We caught the horse thieves."

"You did? How? Where were they? *Who* are they?"

Asher took a seat. He laughed as he spoke again. "Hold on, slow down a bit. I can tell you it was quite a scene. We are not sure how they arrived at David's barn, but we know how they tried to get out. It didn't work though. Behind the barn used to be a road leading out to the old highway. Which it did until last week when it got plowed up so Walker could make the section an alfalfa field. The thieves didn't know this, so they opened the gate and tried to drive out there.

Ruby shook her head in dismay.

"It didn't work," Asher continues. "They sank into the field. With all the rain we had overnight, they sunk in the mud. On top of it all, Radar had them pinned there. No way they could escape. He wouldn't let them out of the pickup."

"What a comedy of errors." She felt anything but jovial. Levi had been shot by one of the men, and this situation was not humorous at all. "So, who are they?"

"They are from another district about ninety miles from here. They couldn't steal there as they are well known to everyone, and the community up there would have suspected them."

Ruby shook her head. At least this part was over, now if Levi pulled through, all would be well.

"With how dedicated the others are praying out in the lobby, it shouldn't take too long to get Levi over this hump."

"I sure hope so. Miriam is fretting so much to get to him."

Asher's eyebrows knitted together; his face became serious. "You do know Miriam saved his life with her voodoo healing stuff, don't you?"

"She told me she tried healing on him after he was shot."

"Well, I spoke to the EMTs who were there last night. They said Levi was dead. No pulse, no breath. Miriam took over, but she wouldn't let the EMTs near him, so they really don't know what happened, but she brought him through."

"We are a healing family, Asher. It is passed down from grandmother to granddaughter. When Miriam and Levi's baby daughter has her own daughter, Miriam will pass it down to her."

Asher sat up straighter in the chair. "What if she has no daughter?"

"Then, the unusual happens. The healing goes to the firstborn son. It continues down the male line of the family, the same way it has with the females."

"Well, all I know is this, I'd want Miriam to help me if I was sick."

Ruby nodded. "She is there for all of us."

CHAPTER 21

After Miriam and Ruby ate their scrumptious fast food, Ruby went to check on Levi's condition. Within a few minutes, a nurse brought Miriam's *boppli* for her to nurse. After telling the nurse she was a midwife, the nurse only helped her a bit with the *boppli*. Each had their fill and dropped off to sleep.

"What are their names?" The nurse asked.

Miriam shook her head. "I do not know. I will wait until my husband, Levi, is awake, and I will discuss it with him. I have some ideas, but I do not want to jump ahead and name them on my own."

"I heard your husband is holding his own. You have a magical talent, Miriam."

"*Nee,* it is *Gott's* will and his healing power to bring people back. It was not Levi's time to go."

The woman placed the babies in their large plastic baskets and wheeled them out of the room. Miriam wanted nothing more than to go see Levi, but she did not know where Intensive care was in this big hospital.

She had enough of the confinement. Looking across the room, she spotted a wheelchair. The nurses had used it to take her to the bathroom. Were Englisch mothers so coddled they had to be rolled about?

Trying to talk herself out of taking a nap, Miriam must stay awake so she could go see Levi. Tossing back the covers, Miriam moved her legs to dangle over the edge of the bed. She realized what a toll the surgical birthing took of her. The wheelchair looked so far away.

Hanging on to the side of the bed, Miriam took tiny, slow steps to the wheelchair. When she finally got there, she dropped into the chair. Glancing at the wall clock, Miriam gasped when she read the time. Nine o'clock. At night. Hopefully, the nurses and doctors were too busy to see her as she made her way toward the intensive care rooms. She did not know the location of Levi's room, but she was determined to find him.

Miriam placed her feet on the metal holders and began moving the chair with her hands. Her arms were much stronger than her legs, which was a good thing because she did not feel strong enough to walk.

Passing by a window, she saw clear, plastic baby baskets. Two of those held her *boppli*. She counted eleven *boppli* in the room. From the window, she could not tell her children from others.

Making her way down the hall, she spotted the elevator. Luckily a guide was posted on the wall directing people where to locate this and that in the hospital. ICU was the next floor up. Miriam pushed the up button, and the electronic doors flew open, causing her to jump. She might own a cell phone, but it was all the technology she used. She was a simple woman and this hospital, with all its energy as workers raced here and there frightened her.

Rolling into the elevator, she pushed a button, and her stomach flipped as the car whizzed upward. The door opened on the new floor. It was not as bright in the waiting room. Looking at the windows, the night sky greeted her. No wonder it was so dim in here.

Looking closer, she took in people gathered near the corner of the room. Most of them were sleeping. Did they have someone they loved in ICU needing extreme medical care?

To her left, a long hallway with windows at each room filled her sight. How would she find Levi here? Slowly, she wheeled toward the nurses' desk where people sat at computers or spoke on telephones. The only way to do this was to ask. Surely, they would not make her go back to her room without seeing her husband.

"Excuse me, Miss?" Miriam said.

An older woman dressed in a large, colorful top with pockets and loose slacks looked over the counter to her. The woman's brows knit together. "You must have the wrong floor, Miss. This is intensive care."

"Yes, I know. I am Levi Miller's wife, Miriam. I wish to see him."

The woman turned and spoke to another woman dressed similarly. After a brief moment, the second woman made her way to Miriam. "Miriam?" the woman said.

She nodded. "Yes, I am. Can you help me find Levi?"

"I'm doctor Adams. I'm caring for your husband. Come. Let's go to his room. How are you doing? I heard you had twins today. I suspect you should be in your room resting, but I understand your concern about Levi."

The woman took the chair handles and navigated Miriam down the hall. They only went past two other rooms where the curtains were closed to block out the hallway, but Levi's curtains were open, and she could see him through the windows. He was pale and hooked up to all sorts of machines.

"Oh, my! My sister told me you said he was getting better. He looks dead to me!" She began to cry.

The doctor squeezed her shoulders reassuringly. "I know he looks terrible to you, but he's been through a long surgery, and now we have him on a medication which makes him sleep. The bullet nicked his heart. I don't know how he made it to the hospital in time, but he did. We repaired his heart, but we are giving him medications to make his heart beat slower and more gentle. We need him to be calm to heal."

"When will you stop the coma medication and bring him back?"

"If his vitals remain stable, as they are now, I can begin weaning him off it tomorrow. It will take a day or so for him to come around."

"Can I go in and sit by his bed? Hold his hand and tell him about his children?"

"Certainly. I am calling down to obstetrics to let the nursing staff know you're up here. I'll give you thirty minutes then a nurse will come for you and take you back. After a good night's rest, you can come back tomorrow for longer."

Doctor Adams pushed her into the room and settled her by Levi's bedside.

"Thank you so much. I will not be a bother."

As the doctor walked from the room, she lowered the bright lights. Miriam sighed. The room felt better now and not so clinical with all the whirring, beeping machines.

"Levi, it is Miriam. I love you so much. Please stay strong and heal so you can come back to us. Our *boppli* have been born. You have a son and a daughter. I need you to help name them…"

She continued murmuring to him, but he did not respond. It did not frighten her, though. The doctor told her it could be a couple days.

All she had left in her was a prayer to *Gott. In the Bible, I have read of miraculous healing, and I believe that you still heal the same way today. I believe that there is no illness you cannot heal after all the bible tells of you raising people from the dead so I ask for your healing of Levi, dear Gott.*

Two days later, Miriam awakened to sunshine pouring in through the large window by her hospital bed. She turned onto her side and sat up. The nurses were allowing her to go to the bathroom unaided now. Walking to the sink, she looked at herself in the mirror. She appeared shrunken. Her cheeks were hollow, and she had dark circles under her eyes. *This will not last forever.* Running a brush through her long hair to untangle it the knots quickly fell out and once smooth, she began braiding it to keep it under control. Standing there in the nightgown Ruby brought to her yesterday was vastly better than wearing the awful hospital gown. Never had she felt so exposed.

Her comfy robe had been destroyed the night Levi had been shot, so Ruby bought her a new one. It was fluffy and soft. A zipper ran from her ankles to the collar. Her sister told her it was easier to keep on than if she just had a belt to hold it together. Miriam supposed she was right, but it would take some time to get used to. She put it on and zipped it up quickly.

Just as she returned to the bed, sitting on the edge, two nurses wheeled her *boppli* into the room. Feeding time again. Miriam loved to hug her babies. She still had no name for them, but she prayed Levi would awaken today. Doctor Adams said Levi was entirely off the strong medication which kept him in a coma.

Miriam took her son, who began fussing in hunger. The nurse held her daughter, jostling her a bit to keep her calm until it was her turn to nurse. Miriam stroked her little man's cheek. It was smooth and warm. What pretty *boppli* she and Levi had created. Feeding him, Miriam dozed off and awakened when the nurse took him from her and handed her daughter to her.

Before the nursing was over, Anna, Wayne, and Asher walked into the room. Their faces were serious. The first thing Miriam thought was something had happened to Levi.

"What? What is it? Did something happen to Levi?"

"No. No, nothing like that," Asher said, "We have news for you about the shooting."

The nurse took the baby from her. "We'll get them bathed and bring them back in later." She turned, and Wayne helped her out by holding the door.

"All of you pull up a chair. You make me nervous hovering over the top of me."

After Asher was settled, he spoke to all three of them. "We have been keeping this hush-hush in the district. I now have the names of the people involved in this horse theft ring, and the name of the man who shot Levi."

Miriam's chest tightened, and it became hard to breathe. "Go on," she whispered.

Anna stood beside Miriam's bed with Wayne standing protectively behind his wife. "The three of them were from Ohio. They crossed over to our districts, stole the horses then carted them back to Ohio. That's why we couldn't find them looking in our areas."

"Why did they stop for so long and make us think it was all over?" Miriam asked.

Asher twirled his cap between his knees. "We think it was from all the commotion of bringing in all the families. With so many people around, they had to wait for everything to settle down."

"So, who are they?" Miriam questioned.

"Does it matter? None of you will know the names from the out-of-staters."

Miriam shook her head. "I do not care, Asher. I want to hear the name of the man who nearly killed my husband."

Asher reached in his pocket and took out a small, spiral notebook. "Ok. The two accomplices are Rowdy Deuel and Herman Grosenick, the shooter was Jim Hooley. He was living in Bishop Eischler's barn, pretending to be a destitute man."

"Oh!" Anna cried. Her legs went limp, and Wayne grabbed her to keep her from falling. Asher moved quickly and got a chair underneath her. Anna sobbed with her hands over her face. "No, no, it cannot be..."

Asher looked at Wayne, his brows knit together, and he tipped his head in the man's direction. "Why is she like this?"

"Anna, I must tell them, dear."

She nodded, and her husband continued. "You see, Anna's maiden name is Hooley. James is her brother."

CHAPTER 22

"Oh, Anna, I am so sorry!" Miriam exclaimed once she could speak. Here sister-in-law's face was pale, and her eyes were filled with sad tears.

Covering her face once again with her hands, Anna said, "I am so sorry my brother did this. I thought my father was the worst person in my family, but I guessed wrong. What could have made James like this?"

Asher ventured a guess. "It's in the nature of some people, Anna. We don't hold it against you that your brother is a criminal. The people of the district love you for who you are, and they will support you."

Wayne nodded and spoke to his wife. "The people around here are wonderful. You must give them a chance. Do not go back to your old ways of hiding from people. Give them a chance to love you."

Miriam had never heard such incredible support Wayne was giving his wife. She was proud of him. Pleased he was Levi's brother. "Anna, I do not hold it against you that your brother shot Levi. You had nothing to do with this. James is the one to blame.

Anna went to Miriam's bedside, hugging Miriam and breaking into sobs. "I am sorry, so sorry! I am afraid for you and your *boppli*. Levi has to wake up, he just has to!"

Miriam patted Anna on the back. "Everything will be alright. This is all in *Gott's* hands, not ours. We must have faith he will see us through no matter what the outcome."

After several minutes, everyone left when the nurse brought the babies into the room for another feeding. Miriam would be glad to be home and set her own schedule. What if Levi was not there. She wondered if she could carry on without him. Chiding herself not to think negatively, she burped her daughter, put her back in the plastic crib, and turned for her son. He looked like his father, right down to the tiny cleft in his chin.

Miriam smiled, then crawled back into bed to feed him.

Miriam was bored. After the nurse took her *boppli* away, she took a long shower and used the beautiful smelling body soap and shampoo. She loved feeling clean, and she became sharply awake.

Ruby brought her purple dress, and black apron to the hospital, On the bedside table, sat her prayer *Kapp*. Today she looked like herself instead of a post-surgery patient. Maybe Levi would wake up when she visited him. She wanted the first vision for him to see her in her ordinary dress. *Dear Gott, please do not take Levi from us, we need him so much. I know you will care for us no matter what."*

She felt strong, so she walked toward the bank of elevators, and once Miriam pushed the up arrow, she had to wait this time. At least she knew where she was going. Today was the seventh day they had been at the hospital. The doctor said tomorrow she and the *boppli* were scheduled to go home.

The thoughts of it frightened her. She will be alone at the house. She was sure she had enough physical energy, but emotionally, she was spent.

The elevator door opened, and she walked inside and was whisked up to the ICU. When she arrived at Levi's room, the curtains were pulled across the glass. Miriam's heart rate increased. All she could think of was that something was wrong with Levi.

The doctor stood at the foot of his bed, and she could not see him. Her heart raced with fear. "Oh, doctor! What is there another problem with Levi?"

The woman stepped aside, and Miriam saw her husband in a sitting position supported by the head of the bed. "Levi!"

Miriam ran past the doctor and to her husband's side. "You are awake."

He smiled slightly. And raised his arms. Miriam gently slid between them and gave him a hug. "I am not hurting you, am I?"

He shook his head. "*Nee,* it is wonderful to take the vision of you into my heart." Suddenly his eyes grew wide. "The *boppli*, how is he, or she? Is it not too early?"

"The doctor said, right on time."

Levi's grin filled his face. "Did you give him a name?

"I wanted to wait until you woke up so we could name both of them."

Levi let out a breath, and his eyes grew wide. "Both?"

"*Jah*! You have both a son and a daughter."

Two weeks later, Asher drove Levi home from the hospital. On the way, the men discussed the horse thieves. Ash told Levi the men were being moved to Lancaster. Lawyers feared the case might be dropped, never to come to trial in Amish country since their creed was forgiveness.

"It is so hard for me to forgive, Asher. I know I am called to do so, but I fear it will take a long time for this to happen."

"I'm glad you came through your surgery. Will you have any long-term problems from being shot?"

"*Nee,* but my doctor wants me to take it easy for the rest of the month. I am going to need help from my brother even more."

Asher turned onto the drive leading to Levi and Miriam's home. Once he stopped the car, he told Levi to stay seated. Then he went around to the passenger side of the car and helped his friend out.

Levi ambled up the back steps with Asher's help. Entering the kitchen, Levi called out to Miriam, and she raced into the kitchen. "Levi! You are here." She pulled out a chair at the table then continued to help him sit down.

"I have *kaffe*. Can I get you both some?"

"*Jah*!" Levi interjected.

"*Jah*!" Asher repeated as well. With an uncomfortable grin.

Miriam laughed. "You are coming back to your Amish ways, Asher?"

He shook his head. "I don't think I could ever come back for good, but I try to help my dad when I can."

Aaric and Bea began to fuss and cry. Levi stood and looked toward the front room. "You have the cradles in there?"

"*Jah,* I want them near all the time."

Asher stood. "I'm leaving you two to enjoy your family. I'm so glad you're home now, Levi," Asher said and gave his friend a hug. "Call me if you guys need anything. I'll take care of it."

"Thank you, Asher. I hope you have a quiet night of police business. You deserve it after all the horse thieving." Miriam said lightly.

Levi nodded, then turned with Miriam to tend the *boppli*. The back door closed, as Miriam and Levi went to the little ones.

Levi looked down at the *boppli*, and they both looked up at their parents. Just their presence in the room quieted the tiny ones. "They must be lonely for our attention, and they know their *Daed* is back."

Levi wrapped his arms around Miriam, and they stood there, taking in the sight of what their love created.

Levi whispered solemnly, "*Gott, thank you for saving my life to share with my family. We will honor you in our home and send prayers of thanks to you with our every breath.*"

THE END

Amish Wedding Casserole Serves 350

Shopping List
28 Chickens
8 Pounds Butter
1 Pound Lard
6 Teaspoons Pepper
28 Crocks of Bread Cubes
56 Eggs
28 Teaspoons Salt
3 Crocks Chopped Celery

Melt butter and lard together in a very large pan. Add liver, and gizzards + hearts (from the chickens) to the butter and lard mixture. Brown and cool that portion.
Beat eggs and add eggs, pepper, & salt to the first mixture.
Add bread cubes, celery & meat to the previous mixture and bake all together, at 250 degrees, for 1 ½ – 2 hours.

Dear Reader,

We hope you've enjoyed getting to know the people of Paradise Wells. The adventures are just beginning, so if you'd like to follow along, we invite you to visit our blog, https://authorspiperandlily.blogspot.com/ where you'll receive special notifications as new books in the Quilted Hills series are released. We also hope you'll consider dropping a quick review at the retailer of your choice. Thank you, and happy reading!

Piper and Lily

BIOGRAPHY

Piper Forrest and Lily Simmons began co-authoring an Amish Romance series in 2018. Best friends, both published authors, used Google Docs to write books together since they live thousands of miles apart.

"Piper" lives in Wyoming while "Lily" resides in both Florida and Maine.

They have enjoyed every minute creating this series for their readers, and they hope you enjoy their books.

Learn more about Piper & Lily

Blog: https://authorspiperandlily.blogspot.com/

Twitter: @PiperandLily2

Facebook: https://www.facebook.com/piper.lily.9469

Editor: Juliette Ashton
Cover Artist: Bev Haynes
All Right Reserved

Also by Piper Forrest

Quilted Hills
In Plain Sight
Amish Heritage
One Amish Autumn
My Amish Rose
Amish At Heart

Also by Lily Simmons

Quilted Hills
In Plain Sight
Amish Heritage
One Amish Autumn
My Amish Rose
Amish At Heart